CONSPIRACY

NORMA A. WYMAN

First Edition

Fulton Books, Inc.
Meadville, PA

Published by Fulton Books 2021

ISBN 978-1-64952-625-0 (paperback)
ISBN 978-1-64952-626-7 (digital)

Printed in the United States of America

This book is dedicated to my wonderful daughters and sons-in-law, Deb and Charlie Beach and Terri and Phil Handy, for helping me through my darkest hours.

PROLOGUE

CHAPTER 1

Maggie Scranton was a widow who was in her middle fifties. She was small with thinning gray hair and intelligent blue eyes. She was a kind person who would help anyone in need. She followed a regular routine every morning. She had a cup of coffee as soon as she woke up while her little dog, Mitzi, waited patiently to be taken out for a walk.

Maggie and Mitzi walked the same route every day, often waving to the neighbors as they were preparing to leave for work. She knew everyone on her street, except the occupants of one house. She believed the house was occupied, but there was never any sign of activity there.

As she passed this house, she was shocked to see a small child sitting on the steps. She spoke to the child, saying she should go back inside because it was quite chilly. The child did not respond.

Fifteen minutes later, as she passed the house on her way back home, she was surprised to see that the child was still sitting there. She decided to stop to speak to her again.

She climbed the steps and sat down beside the child.

"Would you like to pat Mitzi?" she asked. The child did not respond.

"You need to go inside. It is too cold for you to sit outside in your pajamas. Where is your mother?"

The child started to shake violently.

Maggie went onto the porch and rang the bell several times. There was no response. As she started back down the steps, she saw blood on the steps and on the child's bottom pajamas.

My God, what has happened to this child? she wondered.

"What is your name, honey? Do you live here? I am going to take you inside where you can get warm," she told the child.

That was when she got her first response from the child, who started to shake and shook her head violently.

Something traumatic has happened to this child, Maggie told herself. *I need to do something.*

"Then I will take you to my house and make you some warm cocoa." The child did not resist when Maggie wrapped her in her jacket and lifted her up from the steps. It was difficult for Maggie to carry the child and keep hold of Mitzi's leash, but she did not have far to go and somehow managed the task.

When Maggie arrived home, she put the child on her couch, covered her with a blanket, and made the cocoa. When she finally had the child settled with her hot drink, Maggie called the police station.

She talked to Sgt. Paul Tennyson. She gave her address, then said, "You had better stop at house number forty-seven on your way here. You need to carefully check the steps at that address.

Sgt. Tennyson was confused about the call he just received. Why would this woman take a child to her home, a child that she didn't know? Didn't she realize what the situation could look like for her? She could be accused of kidnapping. And what was this about checking steps? *Well, I will humor her,* he thought. Paul was surprised at what he saw on the steps. *This looks like blood. What is going on?* He took a picture of the steps then carefully scraped as much of the stain as he could from the steps and placed the scrapings in an evidence bag. He then proceeded to Maggie's address.

When she answered the door, Maggie put her finger to her lips, indicating silence. She led Paul to her living room, where the child was sound asleep on the couch. She carefully lifted the blanket and motioned for Paul to look at the child's pajamas, pointing to the stain in the back. Then they went into the kitchen.

"You need to explain yourself, Mrs. Scranton. Don't you know better than to remove a child from her home? You could be accused of kidnapping. Her parents must be frantic."

"I don't know if the child lives at the residence where I found her. I rang and rang the bell, and no one answered." Paul believed this to be true. The same had happened to him, but he said nothing to Maggie.

"Let me tell you everything." Maggie explained what had happened to the detective. "You see," she added, "the child had been out in the cold for more than the fifteen minutes I described. There is no way of knowing how long she had been there before I first saw her. I was surprised to see that she was still there when I walked by for the second time. I could not return home and leave her there, could I?"

"No, I guess you couldn't. I will leave the child in your care for a short time longer. I am going to call child protective services then return to that address. Did you touch anything there?"

"I touched the doorbell, then picked up the child. I wrapped my coat around her, so I don't believe I touched any of her clothing. As you can see, my coat is still around her. I didn't remove it because she was so cold. She kept the coat around her while she drank the cocoa, then lay down and immediately fell asleep."

As soon as he radioed the precinct to request a social worker to go to Maggie's house, Paul returned to the building where Maggie found the child. After ringing the bell again and receiving no answer, he tried the door. He again radioed the precinct, telling the dispatcher what was happening, and that he was going to enter the apartment. He walked in and carefully looked through each room.

He was shocked at the filth and disorder in the apartment. In the kitchen there were dishes in the sink with dried food that had apparently been there for weeks. Much of the food in the refrigerator was spoiled. There was little to eat except some cereal, peanut butter, crackers, and stale bread. There was no milk, but there were some juice boxes that had not been opened. The living area had one old rocking chair and a sofa that had probably seen better days twenty years ago, and a television that was televising a soap. The only other room was a bedroom with just a mattress on the floor. It was stained with blood and other bodily fluids.

It took a few seconds for Paul to realize that he was not the only person in the room. A woman was lying in filth in a corner of the room. She was in the fetal position and was barely conscious. Paul tried to talk to her about the child, but she indicated that she had no knowledge of a child. Paul called for an ambulance and waited until the woman was transported to the hospital. He then called his superior and asked permission to search the apartment for anything that would identify who this woman was as well as the child.

He found nothing to suggest that a child lived in that house, but he called for the crime scene unit to come to investigate further. His boss had been able to get a judge to sign a warrant for this search after hearing about the child.

Paul arrived back to Maggie's house at the same time Nell Warner arrived. They entered the house together to find Maggie sitting beside the child on the couch, drinking a cup of coffee. She offered coffee to Nell and Paul, but they both declined.

Nell was in her late fifties, was married, but had not been blessed with children of her own. It was difficult for her to maintain a professional attitude about the abused and neglected children she met nearly every day, but she knew she had to in order to keep her sanity.

Nell gently woke the child, who immediately began to shake, but made no sound. She did not respond to any of the questions Nell asked her. She could or would not even tell her name, age, or where she lived.

"I need to take her to the hospital for an evaluation," she told Paul. He escorted her to the hospital and waited with her to hear what the doctor would say about her condition. He would need that information to file his report about the case.

Dr. Patrick Adams asked to see identification before he would give any details to either Nell or Paul. "The child has obviously been through a traumatic experience. I have no way of knowing if this is the first and only time she has been traumatized, or if it has happened before. I suspect it is not the first time, because of the demeanor of the child. She is very frightened and does not trust anyone, not even the nurse who has been assigned to care for her and who is a warm, loving person."

"What experience do you think she has suffered?" Nell asked.

"She has been sexually assaulted. Penetration may have been attempted, but was not completed. We need to keep her here to determine the extent of her injuries. She was handled pretty roughly, but

I think she just has severe bruises. I see no evidence of broken bones. What will happen to her when she is released from the hospital?"

"She will be placed in foster care while we try to determine who her parents are."

Dr. Adams sighed. He knew that was not always a good option for a child.

Maggie Scranton never saw the child after she was taken from her home. She called both Paul and Nell several times, trying to find out who the child was and how she was. They both claimed confidentiality and refused to give her any information.

After several attempts to get information about the child, she gave up. *I guess I will have to forget about her*, Maggie thought. But she never did.

CHAPTER 2

EIGHTEEN YEARS AFTER THIS EVENT, Carrie Franklin flipped her blinker to the right, took the ramp off Interstate 91, and followed the signs to Bellfield, Vermont. Her foster family told her they believed she was from that town. It seems there was little known about her background. She, of course, had no memory of the town; she would have been very young when she lived there. Research told her that Bellfield had been a thriving community in the forties. It had several manufacturing plants that manufactured items needed for the war effort. Salaries were good, and families prospered. In the fifties, however, many of these plants closed and the town began a steady decline. The town today is just a shadow of what it was. Many of the buildings and homes in the town now are in bad need of repair.

Carrie vaguely remembers living in several foster homes from the time she was about four years old until she was school age. She recalls that she was not badly treated in these homes, but she was confused by all the other children who lived there. Those children moved often. She was constantly expected to adjust to these changes and accept the new children being brought into the home. She did not want to be a part of these families. She did not eat well, did not sleep well, and refused to use the bathroom properly. She would not interact with either the other children or the adults in the home. She just wanted to be left alone. She thought a lot about this later in life. She was sure she was moved often because the families did not want to deal with her behaviors. These weren't families, she thought, they were businesses. People took care of the children as best as they could, but Carrie suspected they were often overwhelmed by the number of children they cared for and by the many problems these children exhibited. There was no love exhibited in these families.

When she was about six years old, Carrie went to live with Jane and Doug Waters. They were foster parents, but refused to have more than two children in their home at a time. The home was quiet, and she was treated with kindness, and she flourished. There was a boy about Carrie's age that lived in the home for the first two years Carrie was there, and then was sent back to live with his parents. Carrie was afraid that she would also be moved to another family, but Doug and Jane assured her that she would remain living with them forever. She did everything she could to ensure that the Waters would want her to continue to live with them. She ate and slept well, she used the bathroom appropriately, and she was obedient. She later learned that Jerry, the boy who lived in the home with her for a while, had been returned to his biological family and had been killed by his abusive father. The Waters suffered intense pain when they learned of the boy's fate. They refused to care for other children. They did not want to suffer that pain again. Therefore, Carrie was the only child in the home from that time on. For the first time ever, she felt loved. The Waters saw to it that she had everything their own child would have had, had they been blessed with one, including an excellent education.

When Carried entered her teens, the Waters insisted she go into therapy. They were concerned about her inability to develop close relationships with anyone, even them. She never wanted to be touched, especially by Doug. She did not appear to be afraid of him; she just shied away from physical closeness. They were concerned that she would never be able to make and keep friends when she became an adult, and worried that she would never be able to develop a close relationship with a man.

Carrie attended therapy sessions for a while, but then she refused to continue. "I am tired of being an acronym," she told the Waters. "The therapist says I have what is known as RAD, a reactive attachment disorder. That means I have problems trusting anyone, even people who love and care for me like you. She also says I have ADD, an attention deficit disorder, but she has no idea why I am the way I am, and I can't tell her anything that will help her understand me better. You are wasting money on these sessions. I am not going to continue them."

The Waters allowed her to stop. They just asked her to consider starting the therapy later, but she never did.

When Pete came into her life, she was sorry she had made that decision. Maybe their relationship could have flourished if Carrie had had a better understanding of her past. She loved him, and she believed he loved her, but he wanted more from the relationship than she could give. She loved being with him, they had a lot of fun together, but she did not allow any intimacy. She didn't even want him to kiss her. When he kissed her, she tried to allow it to happen, but stiffened and waited for it to be over. He tried to talk to her about this, but she could not give him reasons why she was the way she was. He finally told her that he wanted to end the relationship, and Carrie sadly agreed. Their parting was made easier by the fact that Pete was going away to college. Carrie has heard since that Pete was dating a new girl and was very serious about her. This made Carrie sad, but she was very happy for Pete. He deserved a girl who could make him happy.

CHAPTER 3

CARRIE WAS THINKING OF ALL these things as she drove into the town of Bellfield. *I don't even know my real name*, she thought. She doesn't know where the name Carrie came from. She just remembered that the lady who called herself Nell called her that. She doesn't know where Franklin came from either. She pulled that one out of the hat when she went before a judge to have a legal name declared. She thought it had a nice ring to it.

When Carrie turned eighteen, the Waters had taken her to court to provide her with a legal name, social security number, etc. The judge was reluctant at first to go through with this process, but after hearing of her nebulous background, she agreed with Doug and Jane Waters that Carrie needed a fresh start and needed proper identification so she could apply to schools, apply for a job, get a driver's license, etc.

As Carrie drove down Route 5 into the center of Bellfield, she knew her first task would be to look for a place to stay while she searched for a job, then an apartment. After driving for just a couple of miles, she spotted a Motel 6. *I believe this chain is reasonably priced, and will be of decent quality*, she thought. She remembered the "we'll leave the lights on for you" ads she had heard in the past. She knew she would have to be very careful with her money until she found a job. The Motel 6 was situated in a shopping complex that had a restaurant and some grocery and department stores. *This is good*, she thought, *I can eat and do any necessary shopping without having to put gas in my car. I hope the motel has a coffeepot in the rooms. I can buy muffins for breakfast and bread and peanut butter and jelly for lunch and eat in the room.*

Carrie parked in front of the office and went to the front desk to check in. When the clerk asked how many nights she would be staying, she stated that she did not know. The clerk immediately became cool and seemed suspicious of Carrie. She quickly tried to explain her situation.

"I am new to the area," she said. "I need a place to stay while I get acclimated and find a job and an apartment. I will check in for a week then go from there."

"This is a motel, not an apartment complex. We do not usually have young girls staying by themselves for extended periods. If we suspect any problems, we will ask you to leave immediately. How are you going to pay for the accommodations?"

The clerk seemed a little more comfortable when Carrie said she would be using a credit card, and the card processed immediately. "Do you have luggage?" she asked.

"I do," Carrie said. "I can handle it myself."

The clerk gave her the key card to her room, and directed her to the correct area of the parking lot. Carrie was happy to see that her room was on the first floor, and she could park her car right outside her door. She was also happy that she could leave the complex from her room without driving past the motel office. *The clerk seemed suspicious of me*, she thought. *She will probably be watching everything I do.*

After parking her car outside the room, Carrie brought in what luggage she had with her and looked around. The room had typical medium-priced motel décor. It had a double bed, bureau, and a TV facing the bed, a small desk and a table with two chairs. She checked the bathroom and was happy to see that there was a coffeepot there. *I will be set for breakfast and lunch*, she thought. I will eat out only once each day. She noted the fast-food restaurants in the mall. *I will have to be careful*, she thought, *the food in these fast-food places is pretty fattening.* She did not realize that there was a small family restaurant at the other end of the mall.

She quickly unpacked her suitcase, hanging up some of her clothes, and putting the others in drawers. She put her laptop on the desk, then decided to put it out of sight into one of the drawers. *I will have to bring this with me, when I am away for several hours*, she thought.

After getting settled, Carrie went to her car, drove into town, and parked in the town offices' parking lot. The town offices, courthouse, school, and library were all within walking distance of one another. She walked to the library and spoke to the librarian, asking to see newspapers from 1994; she believed that was the year she was born. "Newspapers that old will all be on microfiche. Are you searching for something specific?" the librarian asked.

"I just need to see all the newspapers from that time that are available." Carrie knew the librarian was curious, but she did not feel she owed anyone an explanation of what she was doing.

Carrie was both exhausted and discouraged when she finished going through the newspapers the librarian had brought her. She had been able to skip through a lot of the newspaper, she knew she wouldn't find what she wanted in certain sections. It had taken several hours to read through everything that she considered necessary. She often noticed that the librarian was watching her closely.

When she returned the microfiche to the librarian, the librarian said, "I am glad you are finished with your research. It is nearly time for the library to close. I hope you found what you were looking for."

Carrie simply said thank you and went outside. She was surprised to find that it was getting dark. *I had no idea how long I was in the library*, she thought. *All these hours wasted. I did not read a thing about a child who might have been missing, or for some reason being placed in the care of the state. I guess they did not report that type of thing in those days the way they do now. I will go to the town clerk's office tomorrow and search birth records there. If I don't find anything there, I won't know what to do next.*

When Carrie got back to the motel, she parked her car outside her room, then went to purchase a newspaper and something for dinner. She bought takeout, so she could read want ads in the newspaper while eating.

After looking through several want ads, Carrie finally found something she believed she would be qualified for. It was for a salesperson in what was described as a small boutique. The ad requested that the person apply in person. *I will do that first thing in the morning, then go to the town clerk's office*, she decided.

CHAPTER 4

Jackie Patnode sighed when her alarm sounded. She didn't really dislike her job at the boutique; she just needed to deal with her boss. She enjoyed handling the beautiful clothes she would never be able to afford for herself, and she enjoyed working with the customers. She seemed to have an eye for which clothes would look best on them. The customers seemed to trust her opinion, and sometimes they asked specifically for her to wait on them. That irritated her boss.

Business had been booming lately, and Jackie had little time to take care of the new merchandise that was constantly coming in. She knew that the Reardons had placed an ad in the local newspaper for help. She also knew that no one had answered the ad yet. *I hope they find someone soon*, she thought, as she prepared to go to work.

Rick and Nancy Reardon were difficult to work for. Nancy was critical of everything Jackie did. She never praised Jackie's work, and she was especially difficult when customers came in and asked to have Jackie help them.

She was afraid of Rick. When Nancy was not around, he would comment on her lush brown hair, or tell her that he liked looking into her brown eyes. She was short in stature, and Rick would loom over her as he spoke, nearly pushing her into the rack of clothes or the wall she was standing next to. He often made suggestive remarks to her, sometimes even when Nancy was close by. So far, she had been able to keep him at bay, but she didn't know how long she would be able to continue to do that.

Rick had been a pastor in the local church at one time. Funny way for a pastor to act, she often thought when he walked away from her. The story was that Rick had left that vocation to help his wife with her business, but Jackie suspected that there was more to the story. She just didn't know what it was.

No matter what she had to endure at the hands of her employer, Jackie knew she had no choice but to stay in the job. *I am lucky they would hire me*, she thought. Jackie had considered herself unemployable.

Jackie's past was murky. She remembers little of her younger years. She knows her name because she was in the police ID system. She did not remember having a mug shot taken, or being fingerprinted, but obviously it had been done.

Nearly seventeen years ago, she had woken up in a drug rehab center. She had been brought there by the police. All they knew about her was her name. They said she told them that, but she did not recall any incident with the police. The doctors told her she had nearly overdosed on heroin and that she was lucky to be alive. If the police had not found her when they did, she probably wouldn't have survived. The doctors asked her where her child was, but she said she never had a child. The doctors seemed perplexed but dropped the subject.

When she left the rehab center, she was aided by the people who worshipped in the church that Rick had been the pastor of for several years. She often wondered if that was why she had been given the job at the boutique. She would eventually learn the real reason.

CHAPTER 5

Carrie felt refreshed when she woke up in the morning. She had a blueberry muffin and coffee for breakfast then showered and dressed for her job interview.

She dressed in a blue pants suit that she thought looked professional enough for a job interview. She parked in the center of town then walked the main street until she found the shop she was looking for. *Unique Boutique is a classy name, and this looks like a classy shop*, she thought as she entered the front door.

She was met by a small dark-haired woman who appeared to be very friendly. "Can I assist you in some manner?" she asked.

"I read in the newspaper that this shop is looking for help. I was hoping to be interviewed for the job."

She's cute, Jackie thought. *Rick will like her immediately. I am not so sure about Nancy.* "Mr. and Mrs. Reardon are the owners of the shop and will be the ones to interview you. They will be in early this afternoon. Can you come back then?"

Carrie was disappointed to have to wait, but she said that she would return around one o'clock.

I will go to the town clerk's office first, she decided. *If I don't have enough time to complete my research, I will have to go back, but I hope that doesn't happen. People in small towns tend to be curious about the activities of strangers, and I don't want people getting curious about my activities. I may not want anyone to know about what I find out.*

Nora Ryan was a little surprised when Carrie walked into her office. She knew just about everyone in town and didn't recognize Carrie. She noticed how attractive she was in a little girl way.

"Can I help you?"

"I would like to see birth records for the year 1994."

"What family name are you looking for?"

"I don't know. I just want to scan the records if they are available." Carrie noticed a look of bewilderment in the town clerk's eyes, so she decided to tell the story she had improvised if one became necessary. "I recently learned I may have a cousin I know nothing about. I am just looking for more information if it is available."

Nora did not believe her story, but she had no reason to refuse her request. Birth records were available for public perusal when requested. She got the records and indicated that Carrie could read them in the assessor's office since no one would be there that morning. *I wonder what she is really searching for,* she thought.

Carrie went to the room assigned for her use and immediately spread open the list and the notebook she had brought out in front of her. She was a little overwhelmed when she saw the number of names on the list. She counted eighty-nine, but immediately cut the numbers down by eliminating the names of boys. She then listed only the names of the girls who had been born to single mothers. That brought the numbers down to five. She wrote down the addresses of those five, then returned the birth records to the town clerk.

"I hope that information was helpful to you," Nora stated.

Carrie knew Nora was curious, but she did not want to carry on any conversation. "It was," she said as she left the office. She had time to check out two of the addresses before returning to the boutique for her job interview. She had copied a map of the town off her computer, so she had little problem finding the places she was seeking. The first home she went to was in a typical small-town neighborhood. The homes and yards were neat and had children's bikes and toys in the yard. She checked the name on the mailbox, then looked the name up in the phone book. Two first names were listed, and the first name was the first name of the birth mother in the list she had perused. "I don't think this is the one I am looking for," she said. The second address was now a strip mall. *So much for that one,* she thought, *I have no idea where to search from here.*

Carrie returned to the boutique about five minutes early. Jackie greeted her and told her that the Reardons would see her in about ten minutes.

Carrie was impressed with both Rick and Nancy. Rick was tall and distinguished looking. He had dark hair that was beginning to gray at the temples. Nancy was also tall. She was attractive and well dressed with a tailored gray pants suit with a white blouse and silver jewelry. *Classy people*, Carrie thought. *I wonder why they live in this small Vermont town.*

The Reardons brought her into a small office in the back of the store and invited her to sit down. They immediately asked her about her retail experience. Carrie knew this part of the interview would be difficult, and knew she did not want to be completely honest, but needed to stick to the truth as much as possible. "I just turned twenty but have been out of school for just a few months. I was ill as a young child (she didn't feel it necessary to tell the Reardons that the illness was emotional) and did not enter first grade until I was nearly seven years old, so I was nineteen before graduating high school. I need to work, so I can earn money to go to college." She had already decided to tell them why she had chosen this town. "I came here because it is a small town that I feel I can be comfortable living in, and it is near a community college I am interested in. I hope to take a class or two at a time."

"What about your parents?"

"They are supportive of my decision. They can't afford to pay for my post-high school education. They will help me in any way they can."

"Where do you live?"

"Right now, I am staying at the Motel 6. I will look for an apartment when I have a job."

The Reardons asked her a few other questions, mostly about how she viewed her responsibility to a job if she had one. Would she be willing to complete any assignment, no matter how menial? Would she be willing to work extra hours if required, etc.?

The Reardons said they needed to interview other candidates, review her application, and then they would get back to her. They took her cell phone number and the number of the Motel 6, along with her room number.

They knew they would not have other applications for the job, and they knew why. They certainly did not want Carrie to know that.

Carrie was hopeful when she left the boutique. She believed she had made a good impression. *I just need to wait,* she thought. *Hopefully other applicants will not make a better impression.*

Carrie decided to continue her search of the names she had listed at the town clerk's office. The first one she visited was similar to the home she had seen in the morning, but the name on the mailbox did not match the name of the birth mother. *I can't barge in and start asking questions,* she told herself. *I will move on and see what I discover.*

She was surprised at what she saw in that neighborhood. The homes were all in good repair, suggesting that people took care of their property except for one home. That house was boarded up, and it was obvious that it had not had care for several years. It was badly in need of paint, and several of the shutters needed repairing. She parked on the opposite side of the street and walked across the road to the sidewalk outside the house. When she started up the steps, she started to shake with fear. She quickly retreated back to her car and quickly got in. *I wonder if I have found what I am looking for?* she thought. *What do I do from here? Why would a house I have never seen before make me feel afraid? I will drive past the last house on my list, then return to my motel room and think.*

Maggie Scranton watched Carrie carefully outside her window. *It just can't be,* she thought.

CHAPTER 6

MAGGIE SCRANTON ENJOYED HER MONTHLY luncheon with her friends. She was the only widow in the group, but the others seldom talked about their husbands. The group usually discussed children and grandchildren first. Since Maggie had children and grandchildren, she was comfortable telling about her family and hearing about the other women's families. Her favorite part of the conversation, however, was when town affairs—and yes, gossip—was discussed.

For some reason, the group always sat in the same order. Maggie and Nora Ryan sat on one side of the table, and Emma Perkins and Jane Croteau sat opposite them. Occasionally, they were joined by Jackie Patnode and Nancy Reardon, but that was very seldom because of the demands of the boutique.

After being served their lunch and updating each other on family affairs, Emma spoke up. "I had an interesting visitor at the library the other day. A very young girl, probably about twenty years old, came in asking for newspapers from 1994. I set her up on the microfiche machine with the papers she requested then went back to my desk. I was not very busy that afternoon, so I had the opportunity to observe her."

I bet you did, Maggie thought.

"She seemed to know exactly what she was looking for. She quickly eliminated the sports, ads, national news, etc., and concentrated on local stories. She was copiously taking notes and stayed until nearly closing time. I tried to speak with her when she returned the film and machine, but she clearly did not want to carry on any conversation. She answered me brusquely then went out the door."

"Emma, try to describe the girl more completely. I think she was at my office yesterday."

Emma described Carrie to Nora. "I am right," Nora said, "it is the same girl who was in my office yesterday. She asked to see birth records from 1994. They are public records, so naturally I gave them to her. She had a notebook, wrote down some information, then returned the records to me. She treated me the same way she did you. She brushed off my comments to her and left the office. It was obvious to me too that she did not want to carry on any conversation. She was polite but cool."

Maggie thought about whether or not she should tell her friends that she had seen Carrie outside the old abandoned house up the street from her. They did not know about her experience with the young child outside that house nearly twenty years ago. Detective Tennyson and Nell Warner had asked her not to discuss the event with anyone, and she had respected their wishes. *I am sure,* she thought, *that the events of this week have nothing to do with what happened twenty years ago. But do I believe in coincidences?*

Jane Croteau listened carefully to what was being said. She was always on the lookout for news for her husband's newspaper. *I will tell him what I heard,* she decided, *in case something similar comes up at a later time.*

CHAPTER 7

"Help me with this clasp," Nancy Reardon asked her husband. She was trying to fasten a gold necklace that would match the gold earrings she had just put on. She looked stunning in the apricot princess-style gown she was going to wear to the banquet this evening. She knew her husband would recognize how ravishing she looked, but also knew he would not acknowledge it. Their marriage was a sham, and they had not shared a room for a very long time, not since Rick had been accused of having an affair with an underage girl that attended his church while he was the pastor there. The parents of the girl knew that she was probably as much at fault as Rick, so they did not contact the authorities. They spoke to the deacons of the church, then moved away.

Rick knew he was fortunate for not having to spend many years in jail, therefore honored the request that he leave the church immediately, and promise never to work at another church. It was reported that Rick would be leaving his post to help his wife with her growing business. Some church members were suspicious of this sudden move, and others accepted it without any further thought. Rick was charismatic, and the church members had liked him. Many were sorry to see him leave.

A few months after the incident, rumors of what had actually happened started to fly. No one knew where the rumors originated, but parents became protective of their daughters. They did not allow them to go to Rick and Nancy's store without proper chaperoning.

Rick fastened the clasp without a comment and continued to tie his tie and put on his suit coat. Rick longed to touch his wife, but he knew better than to try. He decided to broach the subject of their interview with Carrie.

"Do you think we should hire the applicant we interviewed this morning, or wait for more applicants?"

"You know there won't be more applicants, and you know why."

"That was a long time ago. People forget as soon as there are other news items for them to think about."

"People in a small town like this don't forget."

"Let's not argue the point. What are we going to do about the applicant we interviewed this morning?"

"I think she may be able to handle the job, but she is cute. Do you think you can keep your hands off her?"

"Nancy, you are being unfair. I have been a good boy for a long time."

Nancy ignored this comment. "We'll give this girl a try, but either Jackie or I must be in the store any time the girl is working. You are not to be there alone with her. Is that understood?"

"Understood." *I hope Jackie has kept her mouth shut*, he thought.

Rick and Nancy were sitting at a table with Ed and Jane Croteau. Ed is the owner of the local newspaper.

"How is the search for a new employee coming?" he asked. He knew a little about Rick's history and did not figure he would be able to find someone to take the position unless it was a woman near retirement age. He tried not to smirk as he asked the question. Nancy was irritated by Ed's condescending attitude. She smiled at Ed and answered in the sweetest voice she could find.

"We were very fortunate to find a very attractive young woman for the position," she said. "I think she will be a good employee and an asset to the store. Hopefully, she will bring in the younger trade."

Ed could not hide his surprise. "May I ask who this person is?"

Rick spoke up. It irritated him that Nancy often spoke up, answering questions directed to him. "Her name is Carrie Franklin. She is new to the area. She chose this town because of its proximity to the community college in New Hampshire. She hopes to earn enough money to begin classes there."

The girls I had lunch with were talking about a new girl in town. I wonder if it is the same girl, Jane Croteau thought.

CHAPTER 8

Carrie was thrilled when she received a call from Nancy Reardon the morning after her interview, offering her the job at the boutique. Nancy stated that they would like to give her a try at the boutique for two weeks. If at the end of that time either party was unhappy with the situation, they could terminate with no questions asked. Carrie was sure she would be able to perform the tasks required of her and would not be terminated. She had no idea that no one else had applied for the position, and that the Reardons were certain they would want her to continue working for them well past the two weeks mentioned.

Carrie dressed in the same pants suit she had worn to the interview when she prepared for her first day at work. Carrie didn't pay much attention to how the women were dressed; she was too nervous about the interview. *I am not sure just how they dress for work, but I will probably have to buy some new outfits*, Carrie thought. *I sure won't be able to afford the clothes they sell at the boutique.*

Jackie greeted Carrie when she first entered the store. "Mrs. Reardon wants to see you in her office. There is paperwork to be completed, then she will explain your duties to you. Please ask me if you have any questions. I will help you as much as I can. The Reardons are not always easy to work for."

Carrie thanked Jackie then headed for the office. *I think I am going to like working with Jackie,* she thought. *She seems very nice.*

"Your primary duty for a while will be to help Jackie inventory and set out the new merchandise that has come in. Jackie is so busy with customers that she does not have time to keep up with the new inventory. Eventually, I hope you will be comfortable waiting on customers and working the cash register."

"I think I could wait on customers now," Carrie told Nancy, "but I would need instruction on the cash register."

"Well, for the time being let's just work on taking care of the inventory."

Carrie worked in the back room of the shop, removing beautiful clothes from their shipping boxes. Jackie worked with her, unless there was a customer that needed assistance. As they worked, they talked easily about the tasks at hand, the weather, and the town. Both were very careful not to talk about their personal lives. Neither of them was ready to divulge any of that information.

As they were unpacking one box, Jackie took one skirt out of Carrie's hands, and she carefully tried to press out a wrinkle. "Years ago," she said, "shop owners would never have put out merchandise without having it pressed first. That is not as necessary now. With new materials, wrinkles are not as much of a problem. Still, I like to have our outfits look as neat as possible when I hang them on the racks."

Carrie was shocked at her strange reaction when Jackie's hand lightly touched hers when she took the skirt from her, but she soon dismissed it as nerves about her first day on the job.

When the boutique closed at six o'clock, Jackie walked to the parking lot with Carrie. "You did a great job today," she told Carrie. "I think we will work very well together. There will be many times we will be alone in the shop. The Reardons are away a lot on buying trips, etc. I will really appreciate having help on those days. I will also help you work with the customers. That is when the Reardons are the most difficult to work for. Nancy has always expected me to be her clone when I wait on customers. She wants me to say and do exactly what she would. The problem is I am not her clone. I have my own personality and way of doing things. That often causes friction between us. She gets really upset when a customer comes in and asks specifically for me. You will have to realize you are your own person, and will not do exactly what Nancy would. If that makes her angry, you will need to learn just to smile sweetly and say you will try to do better next time. That will satisfy her."

Jackie decided not to mention the other problem created by Rick Reardon. *I will only discuss that with her if the need arises,* Jackie thought. *I don't want to scare the poor kid.*

CHAPTER 9

Now that Carrie had a steady job, with a decent salary, she was anxious to move out of the motel. She purchased a newspaper and read through the ads for apartments. She needed to find a furnished apartment since she could not afford to go out and purchase furnishings. At first, she became discouraged—the monthly rental fees seemed far beyond what she could afford. She wanted to live on her salary, and keep the money she had brought with her to help relocate in Bellfield in her savings account in the bank. She needed money to depend on if her job at the boutique did not work out or if she had an emergency.

She read through the ads again, and this time she found one she thought would fit into her budget. The ad stated that the furnished apartment was above the garage at the home of an elderly lady. The apartment was originally a studio for the owner's son who was an artist; therefore, it was bright and sunny. The ad requested that interested parties call for an appointment to see the apartment.

Carrie called for the appointment. After hanging up, she thought, *The lady might be elderly, but she certainly sounds spry and intelligent.* When she drove to her appointment, she immediately recognized that she was on one of the streets that she had visited earlier. It was the street that had the house that was closed up and in bad need of repairs. Looking at the house made her shudder. She could not understand her strong reaction. *I will just ignore the house*, she thought. *Maybe there is another route to the house if I decide to rent the apartment there.*

She arrived at her destination and was impressed. The house was a small ranch-style home. It had flowers, a very neat yard, and was well maintained. She rang the bell. The door was opened by Maggie Scranton.

"Hi," she said, "I'm Carrie Franklin. I have an appointment to see the apartment you have for rent."

Maggie was surprised that the young woman at her door was the one she saw watching the abandoned house down the street a few days earlier. She also fit the description of the young woman her friends from the library and town clerk's office had described at their luncheon. *I bet she is the one who was at the library and town clerk's office*, she thought. "Let me get the keys," she told Carrie. "You can look at the apartment, and if you find you are interested, we can talk."

Carrie followed Maggie around the driveway to a garage that was at the right side of the house. *The garage is as neat as the house and yard*, Carrie thought. She noticed that it contained just one small car. She followed Maggie up a set of stairs that led to the apartment. Maggie unlocked the door, and she and Carrie walked into the kitchen area. The kitchen was small and very compact. It had a table with just two chairs, a counter that had four cabinets overhead, a small refrigerator, a stove, and a microwave oven. "You can see that everything in the kitchen is very small. My son did not entertain here. He just used it as a studio and stayed here some nights when he was working late. He did not need a lot of space." The living area and bedroom were very tastefully decorated with early American furnishings. The apartment also had a full bath, which also housed a small stacked washer and dryer. The whole apartment was bright and sunny and immaculate. Carrie knew she would be very comfortable here. "I love this apartment," she told Maggie. "It looks very comfortable and has everything I will need. I am interested in renting it."

"Then let's go back to the house and talk. I have a fresh pot of coffee on the stove."

The inside of Maggie's home was very much like the apartment. It was neat and clean and furnished in an early American motif.

"Sit down at the table, and I will get coffee."

"I am interested in finding out if you plan to stay in Bellfield for a while," she told Carrie. "I would like you to sign a lease for at least a year. I don't want to have to go through the process of renting the apartment again soon."

"I do plan on staying for a while. I have a job I like and want to attend a community college just over the border in New Hampshire."

I also want to stay long enough to find my roots, she thought, *but I am not going to tell Mrs. Scranton that.*

Conversation flowed easily between Maggie and Carrie as they signed the lease, and Carrie wrote a check for the deposit and first month's rent.

Maggie looked carefully at the check. "I see from the address on your check that you are from Norwich. Have you lived in Vermont all your life?"

"The address on the checks is my parents' address. I intend to open an account in the local bank." Carrie did not want to discuss her past.

"I am sure the checks will clear the bank okay. If they don't, I will know where you live, right?" Maggie chuckled.

Carrie smiled at her attempt at humor.

"Is it all right if I move in immediately? I am anxious to move out of the motel I am staying in."

"Certainly. Will you need some assistance?"

"No, I have only a few things at the motel. I may drive home sometime soon to bring back some of my personal things I miss having with me, but even then, I will not have a lot. If it is all right with you, I will go check out the motel now and move in here."

"Of course, that is all right. Here is the key to the apartment. You are free now to come and go as you please."

"Are there other keys to the apartment? Does your son still have one?"

Maggie was a little angered that Carrie would ask such a question. "No, there are just two more, and I have them. But I assure you no one will enter your apartment at any time without your permission. Do you have any other questions? I have to leave now for a meeting at the church rectory."

"Are there any other ways to get here other than driving south on this street as I did?"

"No, that is the only way to get here. Why do you ask?"

"No special reason. I was just curious." Carrie was not going to tell Maggie that she had a bad feeling about that house.

What a strange question, Maggie thought.

CHAPTER 10

About a month after Carrie had started working at the boutique, Rick and Nancy announced that they would be away for a few days on a buying trip.

Rick had been eyeing Carrie ever since she had started working for him and wanted to touch her. He used this announcement as an excuse. “Do you think you can work here with just Jackie?” he asked as he attempted to put his arm around her shoulder in a “fatherly” manner. As soon as Rick started to touch her, Carrie shrieked and jumped away. Rick was shocked at her strong reaction and turned away, not knowing how to handle the situation. Jackie and Nancy both smirked, thinking Rick may have finally met his match.

“No one has the right to touch another person without their permission,” she said to no one in particular as she left the room. No one mentioned this event again, but all three questioned Carrie’s strong reaction in their minds.

The next day, Jackie told Carrie she thought she should start working with some of the customers. “You are young and have a very quiet, sweet manner. I think our customers will be comfortable having you help them select the merchandise they are interested in.”

A short time later, two handsome men came into the boutique. They were obviously father and son. “That man certainly can’t deny his son,” Jackie said quietly, “they look just alike.”

“Why don’t you see if you can help them?”

“May I help you find something?” Carrie asked the two men.

“My wife has a new navy-blue coat and needs some accessories to complement it,” the older man stated. We were hoping to find something here.” Both men were looking at dark-blue scarves, gloves, and purses.

"If the coat is dark, I don't think you would want something this dark to go with it," Carrie told them. "The dark accessories would be lost against a dark coat. Let me show you something different and see what you think." Carrie showed the two men a beautiful light-blue scarf and a purse with a light- and dark-blue design. The light shade was the same as the scarf, and she showed them gloves that matched the dark blue in the purse.

"That looks perfect to me. What do you think, Chuck?" Charles Warner asked his son.

"I think Mom will love it, Dad. Let's have it gift wrapped."

When the men left the store, Charles Warner said, "That gal knows what she is doing. I am surprised Rick Reardon was able to get someone of her caliber to work for him with the reputation for the ladies that he has. She had better watch her step."

"Maybe she doesn't know about him. She looks like the new girl in town everyone is buzzing about."

"Why the buzzing about her?"

"She seems a little mysterious. She has been doing research at the library and town hall and gives no explanation why. She is aloof and does not talk with anyone any more than she has to."

"She was pleasant working with us. Our conversations seemed to flow easily."

"That is true. I guess she does not want anyone trying to delve into her background or for the reason for her research. Actually, I wouldn't mind learning a little more about her. She is pretty cute."

Charles Warner smiled but made no comment.

Jackie had carefully watched Carrie's interaction with the Warners. *She has a knack for this kind of work,* Jackie thought, *I wonder where she gets it.*

CHAPTER 11

WHILE ENJOYING DESSERT AT THEIR weekly luncheon, Maggie decided to bring up the subject of Carrie Franklin. Only Emma, Nora, and Jane Croteau were present. Nancy was on a buying trip, and Jackie was busy at the boutique.

"Did I tell you I finally rented the apartment over the garage?"

"No," they said in unison. "Who did you rent it to?"

"To a very sweet young girl. She is very quiet, neat, and dependable. An ideal tenant."

"What is her name? Is she from town?" Nora asked.

"Her name is Carrie Franklin. I think she might be the same girl who did the research at the library and town hall. She certainly fits the description you gave of her."

"What is she like? Do you have any idea what she is researching?" Emma asked.

"As I said before, she is young and very pleasant. She pretty much keeps to herself. She will wave hello when she is going to and from the apartment, but still she makes it very plain that she does not want any interaction other than business between us. Surprisingly enough, she works at Nancy's boutique."

"She'd better watch out for Rick if she is working there."

"I would be worried if she was the only one working there, but I am sure Jackie will watch out for her.

"It is quite interesting that both of Rick and Nancy's employees have nebulous backgrounds."

"I am sure it is just a coincidence," Maggie stated.

"There are a couple of things I wonder about when it comes to Carrie. One is that she seems to have an unusual interest in the abandoned house on my street. She even asked if there was a way to get to the apartment other than driving past that house."

As she spoke, the waitress came with the check, and the three women went about the business of deciding who owed what part of the check. After they figured out the finances and the check was settled, Maggie went on to say, "I am worried that Carrie has no friends or social life. She goes to work, comes home, and stays in for the night. She does not go anywhere weekends."

Nora and Emma seemed to forget about Maggie's comment about Carrie and the abandoned house on the street. They were more interested in figuring out how to enhance her social life.

Thank goodness, Maggie thought. I should never mention that house under any circumstances.

As they left, the three ladies had decided that Maggie should invite Carrie to church the next Sunday because a social hour was being held after the service in the meeting room. It would be a good opportunity for Carrie to meet other young people who lived in town.

CHAPTER 12

CARRIE COULDN'T REMEMBER THE LAST time she had sat in a pew in a church. She thought she had attended services with some of her foster families but could not recall when. Doug and Jane Waters did not regularly attend church services.

She wasn't sure if she really wanted to be there, but Maggie had been so persistent about her attending the services and the coffee social after that, that she finally consented. She knew Maggie meant well and did not want to hurt her feelings, but also did not want to get too close to her socially. *She will probably disappear from my life someday*, Carrie thought. *Everyone else has, except Doug and Jane.*

Carrie would have been even more uncomfortable than she already was if she had realized the amount of curiosity she was evoking.

When the church service ended, Maggie led Carrie to a room downstairs that Maggie said was called Friendship Hall. The room was arranged with long tables with white tablecloths. Chairs were arranged, so several people could sit at the tables together. A side table had urns of coffee, milk, juice, and a variety of pastries such as muffins, cinnamon rolls, Danish pastries, etc. Several families were already sitting at the tables with paper plates filled with these delicacies.

Maggie directed Carrie to one table where an obviously pregnant woman was sitting alone. She appeared to be about Carrie's age. "There is someone I would like you to meet," Maggie stated. Maggie introduced the two women when they approached the table. "Nan," she said. "I would like to introduce you to my new tenant, Carrie Franklin. Carrie works at the Unique Boutique," she told Nan. Carrie was surprised at the expression in Nan's face when she heard the news but soon forgot it. "Carrie, this is Nan Wynters. She is a kindergarten teacher at our elementary school, but as you can see, she will soon be taking a leave of absence from her job."

When Nan started to put her hand out to shake Carrie's hand, Carrie turned her head and coughed a small cough, saying, "Excuse me." It was a technique she had perfected to avoid that physical contact without appearing rude. Nan's husband, Scott, watched this activity from across the room. *She has that down pat,* he thought.

Maggie excused herself to speak with some of the other parishioners. "Why don't you get coffee and something to eat, then come back and join me?" Nan suggested. When Carrie returned and sat down beside Nan, Nan said, "My husband is around here somewhere. Perhaps you will get a chance to meet him before we leave."

Conversation flowed easily between the two women. Nan told Carrie about her job, and how much she would miss it when her baby came. "However," she explained, "I will not leave my children in the care of day care providers. Scott and I want to have two children. I will stay home to raise them, and return to teaching when they both start school. It will be an ideal situation. I will be working when they are in school, and will be home when they are home."

Nan soon realized she had been doing all the talking. Carrie had offered no information about herself. In an effort to learn more about Carrie, Nan said, "I understand you work at the Unique Boutique. Do you enjoy the work?"

"I do," Carrie said. Not wanting attention brought to herself, she went on to say, "I think Maggie may be getting ready to leave. Please excuse me, I must go find her."

It was obvious to Nan that Maggie was enjoying conversation with her friends and gave no indication that she was getting ready to leave. Carrie's sudden actions surprised her. *I guess I bored her with my life story,* she thought.

Just then, Scott returned to the table. "Carrie, Nan said before you leave let me introduce you to my husband." After the introductions were made, Scott merely greeted Carrie with a polite "Happy to meet you." *I'll give the kid a break*, he thought. *She won't have to cough suddenly to avoid shaking hands.*

Carrie was relieved that Scott did not offer his hand. She had no idea that he had a specific reason for acting this way.

Later at home, Nan brought up the subject of Carrie. "The girl I met today seems very timid but nice," she told her husband. "I think she has some troubling issues," Scott answered. "I don't want you to get too close to her. She could be trouble."

"Oh, Scott. Once a counselor, always a counselor," Nan teased. "Don't go looking for problems in places where there are no problems."

Later, she would recall these words.

When Carrie returned to her apartment from church, she immediately changed into a T-shirt and jeans. She was restless and needed to find something to do. She looked through the notes she had made when visiting the library and town hall. *I have read through these notes a hundred times,* she thought. *Nothing is going to change. Maybe I am looking in the wrong direction. Maybe I should be looking for the mother instead of the child? But where do I start? I could look through the newspapers again, but if there had been anything about a young mother who could not adequately care for her child, I would have noticed it immediately.*

Carrie decided to go for a walk. She drove into town, parked on Main Street, got out of the car, and started window-shopping. Through the window of one of the shops, she could see the church steeple. She remembered that the cemetery was just a block away from the church. *Could that be a place to start?* she wondered. When she parked at the entrance of the cemetery, she noticed that the roads were well paved. She surmised that people go for walks through there often. She started to walk briskly, so no one would question why she was there. As she walked, she searched for the names of young women who had passed way about twenty years earlier. Even though she ignored the older parts of the cemetery and searched only the sections that had dates from the last thirty years, her search took almost two hours. She found nothing.

Carrie did not realize she was being followed. When she arrived home, she decided not to go inside immediately. *I really need to face my demons*, she told herself. *I can't imagine why I feel so uncomfortable around that old boarded-up house. I am going to walk down there.* She approached the house, but she did not have the courage to walk up to the doorstep. She immediately felt cold and began to shake. She turned and ran back to the safety of her apartment, went in, and slammed the door.

She had been watched carefully by two individuals. *What is her problem?* Maggie wondered.

Jesus, it can't be, he thought.

CHAPTER 13

THE NEXT MORNING, MAGGIE DECIDED to question Carrie about her strange behavior in front of the abandoned house. She planned to be outside walking her dog at the precise time that Carrie usually left for work.

"Carrie, I saw you outside the abandoned house yesterday. Why the fascination?"

"I don't have any fascination with that house," Carrie replied in an irritated manner. She was upset that Maggie had seen her standing there. *I hope she did not notice my strong reaction,* she told herself.

What is the history of that house?' she asked, trying to sound casual.

"Oh, I heard years ago that a child was injured when living there. It was nothing serious. No one seemed to know anything about the family living there at the time, and they moved soon after. I don't know why no one lives there now or why the house was never sold." Maggie did not want to elaborate, and Carrie did not ask further questions.

At work, Carrie could not get the house out of her mind. Jackie noticed that she was distracted by something.

"You do not seem quite like yourself this morning, Carrie," she said. "Can I help you with something? Do you have questions about your work here?"

"No, I am just tired. I did not sleep very well last night." Jackie was the first woman since Jane Waters that Carrie felt comfortable with, but she wasn't ready to discuss anything personal with her. She still did not trust anyone completely.

Jackie wondered why a young, healthy woman would have trouble sleeping, but she decided not to pursue the subject further.

At noontime, Jackie suggested they go out to lunch together. "There is a small cafe just down the street that we can walk to. The food is good, and the service is fast. We can easily be back in an hour."

"I don't think the Reardons will like it if we are both gone at the same time."

"We are entitled to an hour's lunch break, even though we don't often take that time. The shop is not busy today, and the Reardons can easily take care of anyone who might come in."

Once their sandwiches had been served at the cafe, Jackie again approached the fact that Carrie did not seem quite like herself this morning.

"Oh, it is nothing really. Actually, it is something foolish," Carrie corrected. "There is an abandoned house on the street where I live. Something about it troubles me. I have talked to Maggie about it, but she just says a child was injured there, but not seriously, then the family moved away. It seems strange to me that someone would just board a house up and leave it empty for a long time. I am just curious about it.

Jackie suddenly felt chilled and ill. She could not understand why. She somehow got her sandwich down. She did not want Carrie to notice her strong reaction to her comments. *Now who is going to be distracted?* she thought.

He was watching them carefully. *I wonder if anyone else sees what I see*, he thought. *I may need to do something about these people.*

Jackie and Carrie returned to the shop a few minutes before one. They did not want their employers to think they were late getting back to work.

Chuck Warner entered the store about three in the afternoon. He walked directly up to Carrie.

"I want to thank you for helping my dad and me select the accessories for my mom's coat. She was really pleased. She thought everything complimented her coat perfectly. I would like to thank you further by buying you a drink after work. Would you like that? I promise to be a perfect gentleman. I know you don't know me well. We can arrange to meet somewhere if that would make you more comfortable."

Carrie was shocked by this invitation. It had not occurred to her that something like that could happen. She had no intention of dating again. She did not want another "Pete" experience.

"I'm sorry. I am afraid I am not interested in dating, but thank you anyway. You have thanked me enough already for helping you make the correct selections for you mom. I was happy I could help you."

Carrie turned and walked away. Chuck was surprised and a little miffed at the rebuff. He quietly left the store.

Jackie and the Reardons watched the exchange with significant interest.

CHAPTER 14

THE SUNDAY BRUNCH AFTER SERVICES at the Congregational church were held the third Sunday of every month. Maggie had again prevailed on Carrie to attend church then the brunch with her again.

As soon as the parishioners started to gather in Friendship Hall, Nan excused herself, telling her husband that she wanted to speak with Carrie. Scott was concerned about this. He knew that Nan had not had contact with Carrie since the last church social, but he also knew she was planning on attempting to develop a friendship with her. *She is always trying to pick up strays*, he thought. *It is part of her personality and one of the reasons I love her so much, but this new gal makes me nervous. There is something that is not right about her.*

As Scott was watching his wife walk away, Chuck Warner approached him. "The new girl in town is kind of cute, don't you think?"

"I guess so, do you know her?"

"She waited on Dad and me at the Unique Boutique one afternoon. She really knows her stuff and is very professional." Chuck was not used to girls refusing him when he asked them out, so he decided not to mention it to Scott. "Do you and Nan know her?"

"We don't, but Nan has it in her head that she wants to develop a friendship with her. I have some concerns about that. There is something that is not quite right about that girl."

"How so?"

"Well, she is a loner. That's okay, many people are. But if you watch her carefully, she won't let anyone touch her. She won't even shake hands. She has developed some clever techniques that allow her to politely prevent that from happening."

"Maybe she is concerned about germs, cleanliness, something like that."

"No, I think her problems go deeper than that. I think she has psychological issues. That is why I am not crazy about Nan spending a lot of time with her."

Later that evening, during dinner, Chuck decided to talk about Carrie with his parents. "Dad, what did you think of the girl that waited on us at the boutique the other day?"

"I don't know. She seemed nice enough. She certainly knew her stuff, but she seemed a little standoffish."

"Why?"

"Are you interested in her?" Joan Warner asked. Joan had been wondering why Chuck never seemed to be interested in getting seriously involved with the girls he met. He dated often, and she knew the women in town considered him quite a catch, but he only dated casually. There never seemed to be one woman that he was interested in seeing over a period of time. Joan wanted grandchildren.

"Not really," Chuck replied. He had no intention of telling his parents that he had made an attempt to see Carrie and was rebuffed. "I saw her talking with Nan Wynters after church today, and asked Scott if they knew her. He doesn't want Nan to become friends with her. He thinks she has some issues that she doesn't want Nan to know about."

"Well, Scott is a counselor. He would know," Joan stated.

"I know that, but I just don't see the problems that Scott sees. Of course, I don't know her that well."

"Let's try to get better acquainted with her. I will plan a small dinner party and invite her."

"I don't know if she would accept an invitation to a dinner party. She pretty much stays to herself."

"We will invite Maggie Scranton also," Charles said. "She could probably talk Carrie into attending with her. She is able her to get to attend church and the church socials with her, and I can put a bug into Maggie's ear that we would like to have Carrie attend our little get-together."

CHAPTER 15

I WONDER WHY ON EARTH *I accepted this dinner party invitation,* Carrie thought to herself as she followed Maggie's directions to the Warners' home. *I certainly do not want to get involved with any of the people in town. And I don't want to date anyone, so the last place I should accept an invitation is to Chuck Warner's home.*

She was lost in thought and did not hear Maggie's directions. "Carrie, did you hear me say to take the next left? We are almost at the Warner home." Carrie was impressed when she drove up the driveway to the home. It was a very large, beautiful colonial building. The yard was well landscaped with trees, shrubs, and flowers.

"The house is very large," Carrie remarked.

"The Warners have their business here as well as their home."

"What sort of business?"

"The father and son are lawyers, and the mother serves as a receptionist for them. They also have paralegals that work for the firm. They treat their clients fairly, and therefore they are very popular in this town."

For some reason, learning that the Warners were lawyers made Carrie uncomfortable. *I am going to have to watch every word I say tonight,* she thought. *I know people are curious about me.*

When Carrie and Maggie stepped up on the porch, the door opened, and they were greeted warmly by Joan Warner. "Please come right in. I will show you to the study where cocktails are being served. Dinner will be ready shortly."

Carrie accepted a glass of wine as she looked around the room. She felt a little better about attending this gathering when she realized she knew almost everyone in the room. The Warners and Maggie, of course, but also present were the Reardons. Jackie was also there, who she noticed was sipping soda water with a twist of lemon, rather than wine. Nan and Scott Wynters were also present as were the minister from the church she attended with Maggie, and a small plump woman she assumed to be the minister's wife.

Carrie sipped her wine very slowly. She was not used to alcohol, and listened to the conversations around her without contributing any comments of her own.

Joan approached her and walked with her to where the minister was standing. "Carrie, I don't believe you have been properly introduced to the pastor of the church you have been attending. This is John Abbott, and the lovely lady with him is his wife, Maude. John and Maude, may I present a newcomer to our town, Carrie Franklin."

"I have seen you at our Sunday services and at the brunch, which follows the services. I am happy that Maggie has introduced you to our church community," John stated.

"I also welcome you," Maude added.

At that moment, Nan Wynters came to speak to Carrie. Carrie thanked the Abbotts for the warm welcome, and she turned to greet Nan, who led her to the other side of the room.

"Carrie," she said, "we have not had time to really get acquainted. How about meeting for lunch sometime?"

"I would like to, but my lunch hour is very short because of my obligation to the boutique."

"Perhaps we can plan to meet somewhere close to the boutique, so you will have close to an hour," Nan suggested.

Before Nan and Carrie were able to make further plans, dinner was announced. Joan made sure that Carrie was escorted to dinner by Chuck.

At first, the dinner conversation centered around town affairs. Then Maggie turned the conversation to Nan.

"When is your baby due?" she asked.

"In about three months," Nan replied. "We just learned that the baby will be a boy." Scott beamed proudly.

Maude turned to Carrie and asked her where she lived before moving to Bellfield. Carrie told her that she lived just a few miles north of Bellfield.

"Is that where you found out about the lost cousin you are searching for? Did you hear about that person from your foster parents?"

Carrie was shocked that a woman she had just met would ask her this question. Why was she so interested in Carrie's past, and how did she know she was brought up in foster care? She had no intention of answering Maude's question about her past. She did not want her past—or present, for that matter—discussed.

Carrie tried to keep the anger out of her voice when she responded to Maude. "I am surprised that everyone is so curious about my activities. There must be more interesting topics to discuss tonight."

Chuck came to her rescue. "There is. Mom, how about bringing in your delicious chocolate mousse? I think everyone is ready for dessert."

Carrie smiled at Chuck appreciatively. Scott took note of Carrie's reluctance to discuss her past.

Conversation stopped momentarily as everyone appreciated the delicious chocolate mousse topped with whipped cream. But Maude soon continued her conversation about Carrie's activities since she had arrived in town.

"Oh, Carrie," she said, "don't be surprised that I know about your research. Both Emma Perkins, our town librarian, and Nora Ryan, our town clerk, are on the church's music committee. Obviously, we discuss subjects besides what psalms are going to be sung at the Sunday service. Emma told us about your search of old newspapers at the library, and Nora talked about your search of town records at her office, and I hope your search has been successful."

"I am working on it," Carrie replied, then quickly tried to turn the conversation away from herself. "Tell me how you go about choosing the songs for Sunday services."

"That would be a very boring topic, Carrie. We are all more interested in what you think about our town. You live in Maggie's apartment over the garage, is that correct?" The question was rhetorical, and Carrie did not answer. Again, she found herself in the position of trying to turn the conversation away from herself. She still wondered why she generated so much interest. *I am just a little store clerk*, she thought.

John Abbott continued the conversation. "I hear you are interested in a property close to your home on Brook Street. I understand you are afraid of the old, boarded-up property down the street. Do you think it is haunted? Maybe I should buy it and fix it up, so you won't be afraid of it anymore," he teased.

Carrie was getting very agitated. She hated being in the limelight, and she couldn't understand why the pastor was talking this way. She looked at Chuck beseechingly, hoping he would help her out again.

Chuck looked at his mother, who quickly took the cue. She knew that anything connected with doing business in the town would interest her guests.

"Shall we return to the study for coffee? The chairs are more comfortable there."

"Nancy," she said, "I understand you are thinking about expanding your clothing line. If you do, will you have enough space in your current building?"

As she hoped, the conversation turned to the proposal for a new mall just outside the town that would impact small businesses in Bellfield.

Joan had no idea about the impact the conversation with Carrie had on some of her guests. Maggie was stressed by the treatment of her new friend and tenant. She believed that their comments about Carrie and the abandoned house were in poor taste. Some of the guests were very interested in the conversation about the abandoned house. One had been fishing for information, and the other wondered why and was petrified about what might happen next. She was relieved when the subject of the conversation was changed completely. Jackie, for reasons she did not understand, was fighting a panic attack.

The weekend following the dinner at the Warners, Charles Warner, Rick Reardon, John Abbott, and Ed Croteau were playing eighteen holes of golf at the country club. They were waiting at the fourteenth hole for the foursome ahead of them to finish putting, so they could proceed.

"Hey, John," Ed teased, "I hear you're interested in purchasing the property at 47 Brook Street."

John was not surprised that Ed knew about the dinner table conversation at the Warners. Ed and his wife, Jane, had been invited to the gathering, but to Jane's dismay, she had another obligation and could not attend. Maude and Jane were good friends. Ed was sure that Jane had heard all about the party soon after it was held.

"I was just teasing the new little gal in town. Scuttlebutt has it that she is afraid of the house. I hear she is afraid to walk up the sidewalk toward the steps."

"Where would a story like that originate? It makes no sense that anyone would be afraid of that old house. There are no stories about it being haunted or anything."

"I don't know. Maybe Maggie Scranton said something about it to the group of old ladies she has lunch with periodically."

Charles was unhappy with this conversation and ended it by saying, "I believe the foursome ahead of us has moved on. Who wants to drive first?"

The subject of Carrie did not come up again during the golf game or when the men were enjoying the "nineteenth" hole after the game.

Carrie was the subject of a phone call later that evening. "I am suspicious of that new gal in town. The age is about right, and this business about the house bothers me. I don't believe in coincidences. You better plan something that will take her mind off her 'cousin.'" The recipient of the phone call hung up with no comment.

CHAPTER 16

"I CAN'T BELIEVE WE SUDDENLY HAVE two parties interested in buying that old ramshackle property on Brook Street," Barb Barker told her husband, Ben. "We've had it on the market for ten to fifteen years, ever since the bank took it over. In all that time, we haven't had anyone interested in even looking at it.

"This sudden interest does seem strange. Who are the parties that contacted you about the property?"

"One is John Abbott, the pastor of the First Congregational Church in the center of town. He hopes to purchase it at a low price, fix it up, resell it, and make a substantial profit."

"I would be surprised if a church pastor had the financial means to accomplish that. The house has a lot of potential, it is a diamond in the rough, but it would take thousands of dollars to make the house just presentable—say nothing about getting it ready for sale. What are we asking for the property?"

"We are asking seventy-nine thousand dollars."

"I think John would have a hard time just financing the mortgage. Who is the other person interested in the property?"

"I don't know. Someone called and requested the asking price. He refused to identify himself, and refused my offer to show the property. He did say that he thought the price of seventy-nine grand was a bit steep for the condition it was in, so obviously he has seen the house at some time.

"He is probably right. Who owned the place before the bank took it over?"

"I don't know. The Prudhomme family owned it for years, but I don't know who owned it after that. No one is willing to say, but the sale must have been on the up and up. The bank must have done a title search. There is something mysterious about that house. There may have been some sort of tragedy associated with it. No one seems to be willing to discuss the matter. That is probably why no one has been interested in purchasing it."

"If John Abbott continues to be interested in buying the house, go ahead with the sale. Don't wait for this other person to call again. We need this sale to keep us afloat for another month.

The Barkers started their real estate business about forty years ago when the town of Bellfield was prosperous. Their business declined as the town declined. They had only a few homes and no businesses currently listed on the market. Those that are listed will not yield a large prophet. The Barkers hoped to keep the business going for another three years until they reached retirement age.

Maude and John Abbott were also discussing the property on Brook Street.

"Why on earth do you want to purchase that old house on Brook Street? What do you plan to do with it?" Maude asked her husband in exasperation. "The house isn't even livable," she added.

"I think we can fix it up and then sell it, make a little profit."

"And just who is going to do the fixing? You can't even change a light bulb without help."

"Maybe I can get Dan Hardy to do the work. He is a good carpenter."

"Just where do you propose to get the money to pay him?"

"Perhaps he will work for a small fee, and a percentage of the profit when the property sells."

"I doubt that. He has a family to support. You also need money to purchase the property and to buy materials. Where is that money coming from?"

"I don't know. I have not worked out the details yet. I will have to go to the bank."

"John, I can't support this crazy idea. I won't sign loan papers at the bank, or do anything else to help you. We just can't take this financial risk at our ages. I simply cannot understand why you want to do this." Maude left the room in a huff.

No, you can't, John thought, *and I hope you never will.*

CHAPTER 17

Carrie knew that something was amiss as soon as she walked into the boutique on Monday morning. The chilly atmosphere was palpable. She looked at Jackie questioningly. Jackie just shrugged.

"Carrie," Nancy said, "do you recall the pearl necklace and earrings that were on the pink dress with the mandarin collar?"

"Yes, I do."

"Do you know where the necklace is?"

"The last time I saw the necklace it was on the dress."

"When was that?"

"When I left the store Friday night."

"Did you come back into the store over the weekend?"

"Of course not. I would have no way to enter the store."

"Jackie has a key."

Jackie gasped. She could not believe that Rick and Nancy were accusing her of stealing the necklace.

"What are you insinuating?" she asked. "Carrie and I do not socialize. We do not see each other nights or weekends, and I certainly did not see her this past weekend. The only time we see each other is when we are here at the store.

"You have been seen having lunch together," Rick stated.

"You are right, we do have lunch together. But only on workdays, never on weekends."

Carrie spoke up. "I do not like the idea that you are suggesting that Jackie and I had anything to do with the disappearance of that necklace. I love my job here, but I refuse to work under a cloud of suspicion. I will give my notice if that is what you want."

"Relax," Rick said. "No one is accusing anyone of any wrongdoing. We are just trying to find out what might have happened to the pearls."

Rick and Nancy left the room abruptly.

"We better be careful," Nancy said. "We don't want Carrie and especially Jackie leaving us. We would never find anyone else to take their place."

She wished she could be in the boutique this morning to hear the discussion about the pearls.

She was sure that Rick and Nancy would think Carrie was responsible for the disappearance of the necklace. Jackie had been working for them for a long time, and they trusted her. Also, Jackie knew how fortunate she was to have a job. She would do nothing to jeopardize it. With her background, it would be difficult for her to secure employment anywhere else.

I hate to cause problems for Carrie, she thought, *especially if I am wrong in what I believe. However, I do not buy her story that she has come to this town to search for a cousin she did not know existed. And she is about the right age. I have to protect what is mine. My next problem is what to do with the pearls until I can get them back into the store.*

CHAPTER 18

"I AM GLAD YOU ARE HAVING lunch with Nan Wynters today," Jackie told Carrie. "You need to make friends with people closer to your own age. Nan seems to be a good person. I am sure you will enjoy each other's company. I will take my lunch hour when you come back."

Nan was already seated at the restaurant when Carrie arrived.

"I invited Jackie, my coworker at the boutique, to join us for lunch. But she has a regular customer at the shop who often comes into the store about this time every Tuesday. She wanted to be there if her customer came in. She will take her lunch hour when I return to the shop."

Nan was happy that she and Carrie would be alone. She wanted to learn more about her new friend. When she made the reservation for lunch, Nan had requested a booth near the back of the restaurant, so they could talk privately. She was happy that her request was accommodated.

After they had placed their orders with the waitress, Nan sat back and said casually, "Carrie, what is the real reason for you coming to Bellfield? I know you said that it is because you want to live near the community college you want to eventually attend, but there are New Hampshire towns that are closer to the college. Is it simply because you want to search for the cousin you have never met or are there other reasons?"

"No, that is all there is to it," Carrie replied. "Tell me about your kindergarten class. I bet you will miss teaching, but I admire your decision to stay home and raise your child until it reaches school age. You must be very excited about the baby coming."

Nan noticed how smoothly Carrie changed the subject, and realized she was not ready to talk about herself. This was not the time to try to find out why Carrie had settled in Bellfield. They talked casually about Nan's teaching career, that the baby that was due to arrive soon, and Carrie's job at the boutique while they enjoyed their lunch.

When they parted company outside the restaurant, they both had similar thoughts.

I wonder how I can get Carrie to open up to me, Nan thought. *I think she is harboring some troubling issues. Maybe Scott could help her with her problems if she would only open up about them.*

I wonder if I could trust Nan with my reasons for living here in Bellfield, Carrie thought. *She seems to be kind and understanding. The problem is that her husband is a counselor. She would probably share the information about me with him. I had better keep my problems to myself.*

CHAPTER 19

Carrie was discouraged. She was getting nowhere with her search of her past. She decided to call her foster mom, Jane Waters. Both Jane and Doug were thrilled to hear from Carrie. They had been worried about her, but they felt it best to let her go her own way. They knew she would contact them when she was ready. They decided to drive down to Bellfield and take Carrie out for a Sunday brunch.

Carrie had not realized how much she missed Jane and Doug until she saw them at her door. She even allowed Jane to give her a hug, which was a rare event. Doug knew better than to try. Carrie never allowed him to touch her, except for rare occasions when she was very young, and he insisted on holding her hand for safety reasons such as crossing a street or being in a large crowd. He recalled how tense Carrie was at those times.

Carrie had made reservations for them at the small family restaurant that was in the same mall as the motel she had stayed in when she first arrived in Bellfield. She had heard that this restaurant served an excellent brunch. She had asked for a booth where she and her parents could talk privately. She was pleased with where they were seated.

Jane read the few notes that Carrie had taken when she visited the library and town clerk's office. She told them about the sites she had visited, but she did not mention the strong reactions she had when visiting the house on Blake Street. She did not want them to worry about her.

"You have very little to go on here," Jane commented. "Perhaps you need to talk with someone who lived in this town when you were an infant. Have you made friends or met anyone you trust to keep your secret?"

Carrie thought of Nan. "I am getting friendly with a woman I met at a church social. The problem is that she is near my age and would not be familiar with any events that may have happened twenty years ago."

"I believe my landlady has lived in Bellfield all her life. She is a sweet lady, but I don't know if I am ready to discuss any of my personal issues with her."

"Talking with someone who was living here when we believe you did may be your only option," Doug told her. You need to find someone you can be comfortable with. When you do, call us and tell us what you find out. We will do anything we can to help. Now tell us about your job and anyone else you have met."

Carrie told her parents about her job at the boutique. "The Reardons can be a little difficult to please at times, but I really like my coworker, Jackie Patnode. For some reason, we clicked right away." Carrie then told them about the dinner party at the Warners' home.

"Charles Warner," Jane said, "I went to college with a Charles Warner."

"It is probably not the same person," Doug commented. "There are a lot of Charles Warners. It is a common name."

When Carrie, Jane, and Doug left the restaurant, Jane noticed a middle-aged couple coming through the door. *Oh lord, it can't be she,* thought.

CHAPTER 20

JANE HAD BEEN TRYING TO figure out why she was troubled by the people she had seen entering the restaurant when she, Carrie, and Doug were leaving the Sunday brunch a week ago. She thought she had seen the man somewhere before, but she could not be sure. Now ideas were beginning to come together in her mind, and she was disturbed by what she was thinking. She hoped she was wrong, but she needed to find out for sure. She needed to do some research. She got out a stepladder to reach the storage boxes on the top shelf of the guest room closet. She pulled down the boxes that contained memorabilia from her college days at UVM at Burlington, Vermont.

Sometimes you wonder why you keep all this stuff, Jane thought, *but I think I have the answer.*

She found and read an article in the college newspaper about Charles Warner. When he was a senior at the university, he was accused of rape by a girl from the college who was two years younger than him. Even though he proclaimed his innocence, he was charged and spent a night in jail until his family arranged for his bail. After his release, he was allowed to complete his coursework from home, so he could be ready to graduate with his class. There were some minor protests to this arrangement, but the protests soon ended when other matters took the attention of the college community.

Charles was exonerated when a nurse returned to the campus infirmary after being on a short leave and told the authorities that the girl involved in the incident told her the contact was consensual.

She had lied to protect herself from the wrath of her parents if she had become pregnant. The girl left the college and did not dispute the nurse's statement. The incident was expunged from the court records, and Charles was able to move on with his life.

Even though she was disturbed by this story, at first Jane did not share her concern with Doug. She knew he would pat her hand and affectionately tell her she was worrying about nothing. She loved her husband dearly, but sometimes she wished he would take life more seriously. When she finally decided to tell Doug the story about Charles Warner, he reacted the way she knew he would. He showed little concern. "You do not have to worry about Carrie and the Warners. It is not unusual for a college student to sow some wild oats while attending college. As you said yourself, Charles comes from an excellent family and is currently a well-respected lawyer in Bellfield. He has a wife he is devoted to, and they have raised a fine son. That is what is important today."

Jane did not argue with her husband, but neither was she convinced that he was totally right. Sometimes where there is smoke there is fire.

Jane was not the only one concerned about the chance encounter at the restaurant. Charles Warner was nervous about the look he got from the woman who was leaving the restaurant last Sunday with Carrie Franklin. He thought she looked vaguely familiar and could be someone from his college days sat UVM. He hoped not. Of course, Joan and Chuck knew about the embarrassment he endured at the university, but as far as he knew, no one from the community did, and he wanted to keep it that way. If the story came out, or if the people who were with Carrie knew the story, how would it affect Chuck's ability to develop a relationship with Carrie, which was something Chuck was very interested in accomplishing?

Charles decided to call Maggie to see if she knew anything about the couple Carrie was with. Maggie answered on the second ring.

"Maggie, it is Charles Warner."

"Hi, Charles, how are you and your family?" Maggie was hoping the call was about an invitation to another dinner.

"I have a quick question. I saw Carrie with a couple at Sunday brunch at the Star Restaurant last week. They looked familiar, but I could not place them. I wonder if you know who they are. I am worried that I snubbed someone I should have recognized."

“I believe you are referring to Carrie’s foster parents, Jane and Doug Waters. They were here visiting, and I believe they did go to the Star Restaurant for brunch.”

“That makes me feel better, Maggie. I do not know the Waters. Thanks for the info. See you in church next Sunday.” Charles hung up.

Darn, thought Maggie. *No dinner invitation.*

CHAPTER 21

CARRIE THOUGHT A LOT ABOUT her conversation with her parents. *I know they are right*, she thought. *I do need to talk with someone about the real reason I moved here to Bellfield. Maybe I will talk with Nan Wynters. She seems to know the people in this town fairly well. Maybe she will have some insight into whom I could trust with my belief that I was born here in Bellfield and that perhaps something traumatic happened to me here when I was very young.*

Nan was pleased when Carrie called her and invited her to have lunch with her on a Friday afternoon. All their other meetings had been initiated by Nan. When she arrived at the table where Carrie was already seated, Nan sensed that Carrie had something on her mind other than food.

"How are you feeling?" Carrie asked Nan as she sat heavily in the booth. "You must be looking forward to your due date."

"I am feeling fine. I am just getting tired of carrying around all this bulk, and I still have a while to go before the baby is born. How are things with you? I haven't seen you for a while."

"I am experiencing a lot of frustration right now," Carrie answered. After we order, I have some things about my life that I want to share with you.

Finally, Nan thought.

Carrie and Nan both ordered a BLT and iced tea. "Go light on the fries and mayo," Nan told the waitress. "I don't want to feed the boy I am carrying with too much fat." She looked at Carrie after the waitress left and waited for her to speak.

Carrie spoke softly. "I am not living in Bellfield to locate a relative or because it is close to a college in Keene, New Hampshire. Although I do want to attend that college someday. Right now, I cannot think of anything else until I am able to solve some problems that have plagued me all my life."

"I suspected you were not here because of school," Nan told her. "You would be smarter to live in a community in New Hampshire to avoid paying out-of-state tuition. Go on tell me what is on your mind."

"I think I may have lived here when I was very young. I may have been injured or may have suffered a traumatic event that I cannot recall." Carrie went on to tell Nan about the foster homes she lived in and how her life with the Waters had turned things around for her. She also told Nan about Pete and her inability to allow any physical contact between them.

"Scott noticed the clever methods you have developed to avoid any physical contact such as shaking hands without appearing rude when you meet new people. He is concerned that you have some deep-rooted fears that you are not aware of."

"I don't like the idea that you and Scott have been discussing my behaviors," Carrie said coldly.

"I can understand that," Nan replied, "and I am going to be completely frank with you. Scott is overprotective of me right now. He is concerned about your reactions to other people, and he is concerned that it might be dangerous for me to spend time with you. Some people in this town seem to be overly curious about you, and that frightens him. I guess he thinks I could be in danger by association. Would you consider talking with Scott? He may be able to help you."

"Not yet. It was I gigantic step for me just to tell you what I have so far. I need to process all this and see where I want to go from here."

"I have just one question. Do you think I could trust Maggie Scranton with what I have told you?"

Nan thought of the monthly luncheons Maggie attends with her friends and how they tend to gossip. "I think you should be careful about that," she said.

Carrie and Nan were being carefully watched as they exited the restaurant.

CHAPTER 22

JOHN ABBOTT WAS NOT PLEASED when he heard his wife tap softly on the door of his study. She knew he did not like to be interrupted when he was working on his sermon for the next Sunday's service. He was even less pleased when he saw the reason for the interruption.

"Michael," he said to his younger brother, "what are you doing in Bellfield? I thought you were in Cincinnati." *And I wish you were,* John thought.

"Oh, I thought I would visit my big brother for a couple of days. Find out what is new in Bellfield."

"I am sorry to say that you wasted your time. There is nothing new going on here. The town is the same as always."

"Really? I have heard you have a new mysterious resident in town."

"Not that I know of." John did not think of Carrie.

"You are not aware of a young woman who has moved to town? One who is doing research at the library and the town clerk's office? One who visits the cemetery and seems to be afraid of a certain house on Brook Street? Really, John, you must be slipping. You need to do a better job of staying on top of things in this town. I wouldn't want to be forced to divulge our little secret."

Michael got up to leave. "I will leave you to finish your sermon." Michael put his hands up in the air to suggest quotation marks when he said the word *sermon*. "I will be in town for a few days, so I need to check into a motel. That plump little wife of yours doesn't seem very hospitable." John knew that Maude despised Michael almost as much as he did. He hoped God would forgive both of them.

As soon as Michael closed the study door, John put his head in his hands and shook. *What is he planning to do to me this time?* he thought? *Now I really have to purchase that Brook Street property.*

Michael knew exactly what John was thinking. *He will soon learn what I have planned,* he thought as he opened the motel-room door. *I may have to buy the Brook Street property first.*

John Abbott knew exactly what his brother had planned for him when Ed Croteau called him with a troubling question.

"John," Ed Croteau said, "I received a letter today with some troubling news. I think you should see it. How about lunch today?"

"John," Ed said after John had read the letter and they had ordered lunch, "you know I would never print a letter like this in the reader's opinion or any other part of the paper. We never print anything that comes to us anonymously, but I need to decide what to do about the content of the letter. These are very serious accusations. Pedophilia is a very disturbing crime."

John did not want to tell Ed that he believed he knew who had written the letter. He did not want any attention paid to him or his family.

"I suggest you rip this letter up and toss it in the trash. Aren't you at all concerned about the way it was written? Do you know anyone who writes letters in block print? That should have immediately sent you a red flag, made you suspicious of the content. Maude's brother, the accused in the letter, is a high school principal in Ohio. He is squeaky clean."

"Then why the letter?"

"Obviously, someone wants to stir up trouble either for Maude or for me, but I have no idea why. I would appreciate it if we could keep this event confidential. Has anyone else seen the letter?"

"I don't believe so. It came directly to my office in my personal mail. I will keep this under my hat for now, but I need to find out more about Jack Ryan, Maude's brother. Are you going to tell Maude about the letter?"

"No, it would only upset her. Go ahead and investigate Jack if it will make you feel better. You won't find anything that will substantiate what is in the letter."

CHAPTER 23

After Carrie had rented Maggie's garage apartment for several weeks, Maggie suggested that Carrie go to the post office and establish Maggie's address as her own.

"If you do, you can save the expense of a rental box," she told Carrie. "When I get the mail, I will separate yours and place it between your inside and outside doors."

That arrangement worked well for Carrie. She received very little mail: just the ubiquitous ads, her weekly letter from Jane, and her monthly cell phone bill. All other utilities were covered in the monthly rent she paid Maggie.

One day, about two weeks after Maggie started getting the mail for her, Carrie was sorting her mail, dropping the ads in the recycle bin, and putting Jane's letter to one side, when she found a white envelope with her name and address printed in block letters. *What can this be?* she wondered. *I have not given my new address to anyone except Jane and the cell phone company. And who writes addresses in block letters? And who does not use return-address labels these days?*

Impatiently, she tore open the envelope, and she immediately recognized that the message was also written in block print. It had no date and no salutation. It read:

> YOU NEED TO STOP NOSING AROUND TOWN AND ASKING QUESTIONS. YOU ARE STIRRING UP OLD MEMORIES AND CAUSING TROUBLE.
>
> YOU ARE PUTTING YOURSELF IN DANGER. HEED THIS WARNING AND LEAVE TOWN.

Carrie's hands shook as she read the message. *What on earth is this about?* she wondered. *How can I possibly be stirring up memories and causing trouble? And what do I do about this letter?* Her first instinct was to put it in the recycle bin, but soon thought better of that idea. *I doubt I will receive any more of these letters,* she thought, *but if I do, I may need to show them to someone.*

Who would I show them to? Who should I show this one to? Certainly not Maggie, it would frighten her too much. I don't want Jackie involved in my personal affairs, and I don't trust the Reardons. I can't involve Nan. Her husband thinks I may be a danger to her. I can't upset either one of them with the baby coming soon. I may show the letter to Doug and Jane someday, but right now I do not want to worry them. I may have to show it to the police someday. Right now, I will just put it away and try not to worry about it. Carrie put the letter back in the envelope and placed it in the drawer of her bedside stand.

She did not know about other letters that had been mailed the same day.

CHAPTER 24

Jenny Lawrence was looking through her mother's desk, searching for a manila folder in which to place her school report that was due the next morning, when she came across a newspaper article that had been written over eighteen years ago. The date on the paper was June 2, 1995. The page-one headline stated, "Popular Pastor Resigns from Church Ministry." Jenny continued reading the article. It stated that Pastor Rick Reardon abruptly resigned from his post as assistant to the pastor of the Congregational Church in Bellfield, Vermont.

I never heard of the Bellfield, Vermont, Jenny thought. *It sounds like a jerk place. I wonder why mom kept this article. I will put my report away then ask her.*

Jenny went into the kitchen where her mother, Pat Lawrence, was preparing dinner. "Mom, look at what I found in your desk drawer. Why did you keep this article?"

"What were you doing in my desk?"

"Looking for a manila folder for my school report."

Pat looked at what Jenny was holding in her hand. *How on earth did that article get moved from its hiding place?* Pat thought. *It must have happened when I was looking for my list of charitable organizations when I was doing my taxes.* Pat tried to sound casual. "I have no idea. It must have a recipe or something on the back."

"No, there are just ads on the back. Did you ever live in Bellfield, Vermont?"

Pat thought it best to tell the truth. "Yes, your grandparents, Uncle Jack, and I lived there for a very brief time, then your grandfather got a new job and we moved away from the area." Pat tried not to show Jenny how shaken she was over this conversation.

"Did you know this Pastor Rick Reardon the article was written about?"

"No, I don't believe I ever met him."

Jenny could see that her mother was very shaken by this conversation, but pretended not to notice. She wanted to call her grandparents and ask them about their time in Bellfield, and about the article, but thought better of it. Her mother and grandparents had been estranged for many years. They would wonder why she was suddenly calling them with questions about their past.

Jenny could not keep the article about Pastor Rick Reardon off her mind. One Saturday she decided to research Rick Reardon and the town of Bellfield, Vermont. She found an article about a specialty shop in Bellfield named the Unique Boutique. The two owners, Rick and Nancy Reardon, were standing outside the shop smiling for the camera. Jenny was shocked.

CHAPTER 25

Jackie was ringing up her last customer, when she saw a young woman walking into the store. Jackie was surprised to see the woman because she did not have the appearance of someone who could afford to purchase items that were available in the boutique.

"Can I help you?" she asked the girl.

"I am looking for someone named Rick Reardon," the girl replied. "Do you know who he is? I looked for that name in the phone book, but could not find a listing or a home address. I did find that this boutique is listed under the name of Reardon. Does someone named Rick Reardon own this business?"

Jackie knew that the Reardons did not have a landline phone in their home. They just used cell phones for their home and for the business. She did not want to share that or any other information with this stranger.

"The owners of this boutique are away on business for a few days. I cannot give you any information about them or the business. You will have to return next week if you want to see them."

Jackie was puzzled by the expression of strong disappointment on the girl's face as she turned and left the store without another word.

The woman stood outside the Unique Boutique, hoping she could find a way to return the pearls. Their loss had not produced the results she had hoped for. She needed to return them as quickly as possible. She could not run the risk of them being found at her home. She knew Jackie would be the only one in the store. She saw the new girl leave early. As she was contemplating her options, she saw a young girl leave the store, obviously in distress. *I know that person*, she thought, shaking violently. *No, it can't be. The person I'm thinking of would be much older now. But this girl is the spitting image of her.* "Oh no," she said. "Can it be the daughter?" *If it is, why is she here? What will happen to my husband? I must save him at all costs.* Suddenly she realized the girl was speaking to her.

"Are you all right?

"Yes, of course. Why do you ask?"

"I thought I heard you say, 'oh no.'"

"I guess I was thinking out loud. I am fine, thank you." *Well, that takes care of my chances to return the pearls today,* the woman said to herself. *I don't want the girl to remember seeing me enter the store.* She walked down the street without another word.

Are all the people in this town weird? Jenny asked herself.

Jackie soon forgot about the incident at the boutique. She had no idea of the drama that had played outside the store after the young girl left. She had other things to think about. What was the meaning of the disturbing letter she had received in the mail yesterday? It was written in block print and said:

> DON'T GET TOO COZY WITH THE NEW GIRL AT THE SHOP.
>
> SHE MAY BE TROUBLE. SHE MAY BRING BACK THE PAST.
>
> BELIEVE ME, YOU DO NOT WANT THAT TO HAPPEN.

*****

She thought she heard a cry. What was it? A cat mewling? Another animal in distress? She needed to ignore the sound. It had nothing to do with her. She could not help whatever it was that was in distress. She was so sick, so tired. Where was she? "No, no, don't do that to my arm again!" she screamed, then all went black.

Jackie awoke bathed in sweat and shaking. She thought she was through with these dreams.

CHAPTER 26

Jackie simply could not concentrate on her work. Who wrote that letter? Who was the girl who came into the store, then left so abruptly? What is triggering the onset of the dream? She thought she was done having those dreams. It had been months since she had the last one. What ideas try to come into her thoughts when she thinks about the girl? Why can't she remember them, deal with them? *They seem to fade away as soon as they surface. I need to talk with someone*, Jackie thought.

Jackie suddenly realized that Carrie was speaking to her.

"Are you okay, Jackie? You seem a bit distracted. I need to know where you want these new dresses to be displayed."

"I'm fine," Jackie answered. "I just feel a little out of sorts. I hope I am not coming down with something. Why don't you decide where to display the dresses? You have a good eye for that type of work. I am sure you will do a fine job."

Carrie was thrilled to have the opportunity to set up her own display of dresses. She had been waiting for a long time for the opportunity to display her skills, but at the same time she was very worried about Jackie. She looked pale and tired and definitely was not herself today.

As soon as Carrie got busy with her new task, Jackie stepped into the office to use the phone. She didn't think that local calls were recorded on the phone bills; she certainly hoped they were not.

Maude Abbott picked up the phone. "Rectory."

"Hello?" Jackie said timidly. "I am not a regular parishioner in your church, but I need to talk with someone about some difficulties I am experiencing. I wondered if I could make an appointment to speak with Pastor Abbott."

"I am sure Pastor Abbott will be happy to speak with you. If he does not feel he can help you, with your permission, he will refer you to someone who can. May I ask your name?

"Jackie Patnode."

Maude tried not to audibly gasp when she heard the name. "When is a convenient time for you to meet with the pastor?"

"I don't leave work until after 5:00 p.m. each day. I could take a lunch break at one o'clock someday and come in then."

"Does Thursday at one o'clock work for you?

"That is a good time."

"Great. And please feel free to bring your lunch with you. You can eat and talk at the same time. Pastor Abbott would not want you to miss your lunch."

"Thank you. See you Thursday."

Maude could not wait to go into John's office and tell him the name of the person he would be meeting with on Thursday. "John, I just made an appointment for you to meet with someone on Thursday. She seems to be under a lot of stress and needs to discuss her problems with someone. I told her to feel free to bring her lunch with her, so I will serve you your lunch at the same time. You can sit in the wing chairs with the coffee table between you. That way, both of you should feel comfortable, and conversation should flow easily as you eat lunch. Oh, by the way, the name of your visitor is Jackie Patnode."

She smiled as she saw her husband turn pale. She turned and left the room, still smiling.

CHAPTER 27

JACKIE WAS NERVOUS ABOUT HER meeting with John. She wasn't sure how much of her past she wanted to reveal to him. Did she want to tell him that there was a large chunk of her life that she could not recall, that that chunk was several years long? She recalled nothing of her life before she woke up one morning in a rehab facility.

At that time, she began her long road to recovery from drug addiction. When she was released from the rehab center, she had a job offer. She had no idea why she was offered the position at the Unique Boutique in Bellfield, Vermont, but she was eternally grateful for the opportunity to work.

She was still pondering what to say to John when Maude ushered her into the rectory. John stood up and shook her hand, welcoming her kindly. Maude noticed that Jackie had brought just a sandwich with her, and offered her a cup of coffee to go with it. Jackie gratefully accepted the offer.

After bringing Jackie her coffee and a plate for her sandwich, Maude left the room, quietly closing the door.

John noticed Jackie's reticence to start a conversation. "Just relax and have your coffee and sandwich," he told her. "Talk when you feel comfortable doing so." He sipped his coffee and waited patiently for Jackie to speak.

"I guess," Jackie said tentatively, "I will start by showing you a letter I received, and telling you about a young girl who recently visited the boutique." She handed the letter to John to read. John was startled when he saw what he believed to be Michael's handiwork. He tried to appear nonchalant as Jackie went on to tell him about receiving the letter, about the young girl's visit to the boutique, and how her visit triggered something in her mind that she could not grab hold of, and about her recurring dreams.

"What do you believe brings on these dreams?" John asked.

He listened carefully as she explained that she had no memory of her past. "I don't know if these dreams are related to something from my past that I know nothing of."

"Jackie," John said, "I think you need to recover those lost years. I don't think I have the skills necessary to help you do that. You need to see someone who has more professional training than I do. Do you know Scott Wynters?"

"No, I know of a Wynter who is becoming a friend of my coworker. They occasionally have lunch together. I don't know if they are related."

"Nan is Scott's wife."

"I don't know if I want to talk with someone who has a connection with my acquaintances. I am a very private person."

"The fact that you are seeing a counselor ensures that anything you tell that person will be kept confidential. You need to think seriously about my suggestion."

Jackie looked at her watch. "My, it is getting late. I need to return to work." She pulled out her checkbook. "What do I owe you for this visit?"

"Absolutely nothing. The church pays me for my time. You can repay me by attending church sometime, and think carefully about my suggestion that you see Scott Wynters."

Jackie thanked John profusely and left the rectory.

As soon as Jackie was gone, Maude came into the office.

"Don't think about asking me any questions, Maude. You know my work in here is confidential."

Maude left disappointed

John picked up the phone.

It had been a very busy morning at the boutique. Carrie had done most of the work because Jackie was distracted and not thinking. *I have never seen her like this before,* Carrie thought. *I wonder what is going on.*

Jackie could not concentrate when she returned to work after meeting with John and went home early, leaving Carrie to close up.

Carrie was very tired when she got home from work. *I have dinner planned for tonight,* she thought, *but I think I will take myself out for dinner tomorrow night.*

She did not know the impact this decision would have on her life.

CHAPTER 28

CARRIE TRIED TO IGNORE THE stares of the other diners when she asked the hostess for seating for a party of one. She was seated in the back of the dining room at a small table for two, which the hostess usually reserved for couples that she sensed wanted to be alone. *It is early, and she won't be here long,* the hostess thought. *The table will be available soon if I need it.*

Carrie declined the offer of a cocktail and ordered the scallop dinner. That was why she was here. Sometimes she just wanted a meal that she could not prepare for herself at home. The scallops that could be purchased in the frozen food department of the local supermarket were not palatable. Besides, she had promised to take herself out to dinner tonight after the hectic day at work yesterday.

Chuck Warner seldom dined out with his parents when they were dining with another couple. He felt like the fifth wheel. However, his dad had prevailed on him to join them this evening. The other couple were potential clients. Chuck was perusing the menu when he saw Carrie walk by. Charles Warner saw her too, and saw the longing in Chuck's eyes. He patted his wife's arm then pointed, so she would understand his next words.

"Chuck, I believe I just saw a potential client walk by. You might want to go over and say hello. If you choose to stay and have dinner with the client, go ahead. I am sure the Bardens will understand." The Bardens were happy to agree. *Just one person questioning me,* Mr. Barden thought.

Carrie did not see Chuck approach. She was busy reading the place mat that listed points of interest in and around Bellfield. That way she could avoid the curious looks coming her way from the other diners. She was startled when she heard Chuck speak.

"May I join you? You could save me from a long, boring dinner of lawyers with my parents and their guests."

Carrie was warmed by Chuck's boyish grin. She threw caution to the wind. "I wouldn't want you to be bored at dinner, but I am not sure I won't be just as boring."

"Let me be the judge of that. Can I buy you a drink? he asked as the hostess brought his drink that his father had sent to Carrie's table. Carrie declined, and Chuck ordered his dinner, also the scallops.

"Would you like me to hold your dinner, so they can be brought out at the same time?" the hostess asked Carrie.

Carrie nodded. "You can give me the fresh dinner, and him the holdover," she said playfully.

What on earth am I thinking of? she thought. *I am never playful like this. I need to remember Pete and be very careful.*

Chuck also noticed her playfulness and thought, *This could be an interesting dinner.*

The conversation between Chuck and Carrie flowed easily as they waited for their dinners. They discussed their work, town affairs, and the local football team. Neither discussed personal issues.

When they finished their dinners, Chuck ordered chocolate cake. Carrie declined dessert, but she said she would have coffee to keep Chuck company, while he enjoyed the cake. She refused Chuck's offer to pay for the dinners. Dutch treat, she said.

Chuck did not argue. He felt he had made good progress with Carrie and did not want to spoil their pleasant evening together. *Next time, I will offer a movie,* he thought. He was confident there would be a next time.

When they left the restaurant, Chuck walked Carrie to her car and waited until she was safely buckled up and locked in. He waved and watched wistfully as she drove away.

Interesting, the observer thought.

CHAPTER 29

IT HAD NOT BEEN A good day for John Abbott. At breakfast, he and Maude had had an argument about purchasing the Brook Street property. He did not like starting the day by having a disagreement with his wife. He loved her dearly and wanted his marriage to be harmonious. He had always been open and honest with her about everything except the mistake he made about eighteen years ago. No one knew about that except Michael. Michael learned about it when he overheard a phone call John had made to a parishioner. Michael had held that knowledge over John's head ever since.

Still upset over his disagreement with Maude, John had called Michael at the motel where he was staying, only to discover that his brother had checked out earlier that morning. He tried to call Michael on his cell phone, but got a message that Michael was driving and couldn't answer the phone. "Leave a message with a phone number, and I will get back to you as soon as possible," the message stated. *I'm sure you will,* John thought.

John's next stop was Barden's Real Estate Office. He wanted to determine the exact price of the property on Brook Street before he went to the bank to apply for a loan. "What do you mean the property is under contract? Who is buying it?"

"I don't know," Ben Barden answered. "The transaction is being handled by a bank in Massachusetts. The party interested in the property wants to remain anonymous. The bank assures me that the transaction is perfectly legal. It is not unusual to have a bank or a lawyer to handle these kinds of contracts for a third party. I am confident that everything is on the up and up."

John did not want Ben to see how upset he was about the potential sale of the property, so he prepared to leave the office quickly. "If the sale falls through, please let me know," he told Ben as he went out the door.

Why would someone out of town be interested in that old, run-down house? he wondered. *Does anyone besides Michael and me know its history? I thought at the time I was doing what was best for everyone, but in retrospect I know I should have handled things differently.*

John had mixed feelings when his phone rang and his caller ID told him that Michael was returning his call. He hated the idea of talking to Michael, but knew he must.

"You looking for me?" Michael asked when John picked up the phone.

"Yes, I want to know what you hoped to accomplish when you wrote those letters."

"What letters?"

"The ones you wrote to Ed Croteau and a woman named Jackie Patnode. You must have realized that Ed would not print a letter written anonymously. The letter cannot serve any purpose."

"John, I did not write any letters."

"Do you really expect me to believe that? You threatened to divulge to the public the events that happened years ago. I did not think you would stoop so low as to involve innocent people in your scheme just because you want to hurt me."

John hung up without waiting for a reply.

I hope this day does not get any worse, John thought as he headed home. *There is one positive note to the day. Maude will be very happy when I tell her I probably will not be purchasing the Brook Street property.*

CHAPTER 30

NELL WARNER SIGHED AS SHE put her last folder in the file cabinet. At least this case has a happy ending, she thought to herself. A beautiful little baby has been adopted into a loving family before suffering neglect or even worse abuse. The judge recognized that the young girl that gave birth to the child, and the young man believed to be the child's biological father, would not be able to give her adequate care. As soon as he was provided proof of their drug addiction, that they had no home to bring the child to, and no visible means of support, he the signed the petition Nell brought to him terminating the couple's parental rights. Soon after, he signed adoption papers placing the child with a young professional couple who was not able to have children of their own.

Nell had worked as a social worker at DCYF for thirty years. She knew it was time for her to retire, and she had no regrets about her decision to do so.

What she did have regrets about, and would have for the rest of her life, were the times the system failed the children. She regretted the number of times the department did not discover the abuse and neglect of children until it was too late. She regretted the times that social workers did not do a thorough enough investigation, therefore failing to remove children from situations no child should have to endure. And she was especially angry at the judges who sided with the parents even though the social workers provided strong evidence that their children were being abused and neglected. She especially remembered one case that involved a beautiful little boy about seven years old. He was placed with a loving foster family. The parents petitioned the courts to have their parental rights restored. The dad cried, saying how much he missed his son, that he was in counseling, and was taking an anger-management class, and would be able to be a good dad to the boy. The mother concurred and said she wanted her child to be returned home. Nell's pleas to the judge that returning the child to his home would put the child in imminent danger fell on deaf ears, and the boy was returned to the parents. Within a few weeks the boy was killed by his father while in a drunken rage. The foster family the little boy lived with before being returned to his parents was devastated by the news of the child's death. They consented to keep the little girl who was currently in their care, but they refused to take in other foster children. Their contempt for the system was palpable.

Nell had tears in her eyes as she put on her coat to leave her office for the last time. She had stayed late to be sure all her files were in order for the new person taking her place the next day. *I just hope my replacement will do a good job*, she thought. Just as she was closing her office door for the final time, the phone in the reception area rang. It was six o'clock, and everyone else had left about an hour earlier, so there was no one else there to answer a call. Nell was tempted to let it ring, but she feared that the call was an emergency call about a child. *If something happens to a child because I don't pick up the phone*, I will never forgive myself.

"Department of Child Services."

"I am calling to find information about a case that is about twenty years old," the caller stated. I believe the child lived on Brook Street and may have been abused."

"I cannot give out any information about a child," Nell informed the caller.

"I am a lawyer and need the information immediately," the caller stated.

"If you were a lawyer, you would know that no such information about any child can be provided without going through the proper channels. The request probably would require a warrant signed by a judge. I don't know what your agenda is, but you will receive no assistance from this office over the phone."

Nell hung up. *Why does that voice seem familiar?* she thought.

Oh well, I tried, the caller said to himself as he also hung up the phone.

CHAPTER 31

CARRIE RECOGNIZED THE ENVELOPE AS soon as she saw it while going through her mail. Her fingers trembled as she opened the flap on the envelope. It simply said:

WHY ARE YOU STILL IN TOWN? DO YOU WANT PEOPLE AROUND YOU TO GET HURT?

Who am I putting in danger? Carrie wondered. *Certainly not Maggie. If I thought I was putting her in danger by living here in her garage apartment, I would have to move. Where would I go, and what reason would I give Maggie for moving?*

What about Nan? I have a date to have lunch with her today. I will show her the letters and will explain that I can no longer meet her for lunch for her own safety. I know her husband will agree with my decision. He worries all the time about her and the baby's safety. Nan gets a kick out of him being so concerned. I don't think I am putting Jackie or the Reardons in danger. We just have a professional relationship.

Later that day, during lunch, Carrie showed Nan the letters and explained that, because of the letters, it was necessary to stop their luncheon dates. "You have become a dear friend," Carrie told Nan. "Maybe when the mystery of the letters is solved, we can resume our friendship."

"I would like that," Nan said. "I would also like to keep these letters and show them to Scott."

"I don't know, Nan, I may want to show the letters to the police if I continue to receive them. I don't want anything to happen to them."

"I am going to meet Scott in an hour. He is accompanying me to my regular monthly checkup at the doctor's office. I will have him read the letters then immediately put them in his office safe. You really need to share the letters with someone like Scott who is in a position to help you."

"Okay, I will take a chance and let you keep them. I really appreciate all that you have done for me. I am thinking seriously about seeing Scott. Thank you for being patient with me while I try to make this difficult decision. I need to get back to work now. Jackie has not been herself lately, so I am doing the bulk of the work."

He watched as Nan and Carrie left the restaurant. *I hope Carrie is not sharing the letters with Nan,* he thought. *I would hate to hurt a woman so late in her pregnancy.*

CHAPTER 32

HE HAD NO IDEA WHY Jackie Patnode went to see John Abbott. He was fortunate that he happened to be driving by the rectory just as she was leaving, or he would not have known about the visit. *Someone up there likes me,* he thought sarcastically. The visit may have been innocuous, but he could not take any chances. Time to get her nervous again.

Jackie knew she had to do something. She knew that everyone at work was noticing the change in her. The second letter had frightened her more than the first. It was written in block print like the first. She was sure it was from the same person. It said:

> WHY DID YOU VISIT JOHN ABBOTT?
> WHAT DID YOU DISCUSS WITH HIM?
> I WARNED YOU NOT TO DIG UP THE PAST REMEMBER, I AM WATCHING YOU.
> I KNEW ABOUT YOUR VISIT TO JOHN ABBOTT DIDN'T I?

Jackie decided to call the rectory. She was nervous about the fact that Mrs. Abbott knew about her calls, and visits, but realized there was little she could do about it. As soon as John answered, she identified herself, hoping no one else was listening to her call.

"I need help," she said. "I received another threatening letter, but I cannot bring it to you because I am being watched."

"What makes you think you are being watched? How would you know that?"

"Let me read the contents of the letter to you."

John listened carefully as Jackie read the letter. "Maybe this should be reported to the police," John suggested.

"No, I am not ready to do that. I want to take your advice and talk to Scott Wynters, but how can I do that if someone is watching my every move?"

"Let me call Scott and see what we can come up with. I will call you back."

John called Scott as soon as he hung up from talking to Jackie. He told Scott about Jackie's visit and the phone call. "She is afraid to make an appointment to see you because she is being watched."

"Let me think about how I can solve this problem, then I will get back to you," Scott told John.

What is happening in this town? Scott wondered. *Is it a coincidence that both women are receiving letters regarding their pasts? I don't really believe in coincidences, but I don't believe there is any way they can be connected. The only connection the two have is that they work at Unique Boutique. I will figure out a way to see Ms. Patnode.*

Nan thinks Carrie is considering starting regular sessions with me. It was difficult for Carrie to tell Nan about the letters, and even more so to let Nan tell me about them, but her letters are really scaring her. I hope she starts the sessions soon. These two counseling sessions may get very interesting.

CHAPTER 33

A FEW DAYS AFTER SPEAKING WITH John Abbott about a counseling session with Jackie Patnode, Scott settled on a plan to get her to his office without being detected by anyone who may be watching her. *It seems like foreign intrigue, but it may work*, he thought. Once he had the plan formalized in his mind, he called Jackie.

"Jackie, this is Scott Wynters. I may have a way I can meet with you without us having to worry about you being detected by anyone who may be watching you. This plan seems a little out of the ordinary, but I think it will work. Tell me if it doesn't work for you. I suggest you drive to the mall and enter through the south entrance near the supermarket. Browse through the stores for a few minutes, carefully checking your surroundings. When you feel comfortable that you are not being watched, make your way to east entrance, and I will pick you up there and we can drive to my office. After our meeting, we will reverse the plans to get you safely home. We should meet as soon as you leave work, so you can get home before dark. I don't want you to feel afraid."

"I don't think I will be afraid."

"Good! Will next Monday right after five work for you? Once you are at the mall, we can keep in contact through our cell phones, so I will know just what time to pick you up at the east entrance. No one will pay attention to someone taking on the phone. Most people are on their phones all day."

"Monday is a good day. We are not usually busy at the boutique on Mondays, so I should be able to leave work right on time."

Jackie was jumpy all day on Monday. She was nervous about her meeting with Scott and almost wished she had not made the appointment. I have to go to this meeting. I have to find out what the writer is alluding to when he mentions my past. I need to find those lost years. Then maybe I can find some peace."

As soon as the boutique was closed Monday night, Jackie hurried out the door and ran to her car in the parking lot. She has been more aware of her surroundings since she started receiving the letters. She did not see anyone nearby, or any other evidence that she was being watched, but she still drove around the main streets before driving to the mall. She checked her rear- and side-door mirrors frequently before driving into the mall parking lot. She was convinced she was not being followed. She parked as close as possible to the mall's south entrance. Once inside, she spent a few moments window-shopping, then called Scott and told him she would be at the east entrance in about five minutes.

Except for a brief greeting, Jackie and Scott did not converse until they arrived at Scott's office. Once there, Scott hung up Jackie's jacket and offered her coffee, which she declined. *I am so nervous I couldn't even keep coffee down*, she thought.

Once they were settled, Scott spoke. "Tell me about yourself, Jackie," he said.

"My recollections of my life are very vague. Except for the few months I was in rehab in Burlington, I don't recall anything about my life. I believe I lived here in Bellfield before I went to rehab, otherwise why would I have been offered a job here?"

"Do you know where your parents are? Do you have siblings?"

"I have no idea."

"I will do some research and try to locate them. They must be worried about you."

"There is no way to do that."

"Why?"

"Because I do not know their names."

"It can't be too hard to find a Patnode family that lived in Bellfield a few years ago."

"You do not understand. I do not know what my real name is."

"How did you get the name you have now?"

"It was written on a piece of paper that was taped to my clothes when I was taken to the hospital. I don't know how it got there."

"I will contact the local schools and go through town records to see if I can find anything about a Patnode family. That would be helpful."

"You don't understand. The counselors and administrators at the rehab center have already done that. There is no record of a Jackie Patnode in the school system during the years I would have attended schools here. There is no information about a Patnode I could have been connected with. The truth is, I am here, but I don't exist."

Scott was totally confused. "I will go to the town offices and newspaper and do my own research," he decided.

The man chuckled as he watched Jackie Patnode leave the mall and get into her car and drive home to her apartment. *I thought Scott Wynters was an intelligent man,* he thought. *Did he really think this little subterfuge would work?*

Time to make Jackie Patnode disappear again. This time I will do better job.

CHAPTER 34

Pat Lawrence went up to Jenny's room and knocked. "Jen, can I come in?"

"Sure, Mom, I am just doing homework."

Pat got right to the point for her visit. "Where did you go with the car on Saturday?"

"I told you. I went to Marcie's house to work on our report on the Constitution. We needed more information for the report, so we went to the library to do research. When that was done, we went back to Marcie's house. Marcie's mother went shopping, so if you tried to call, no one would have answered the phone."

"What library did you go to?"

Jenny looked at her mother, puzzled. "The town library, of course. What are you talking about?"

"I did call Marcie's house to see if you wanted to go out to dinner with me and some of my friends that evening. Marcie's mother was not shopping, and Marcie was not at the library with you. They said they had not seen you all that day. I checked the mileage on the car, and it was one hundred miles over what it should have been. That tells me you drove fifty miles somewhere and fifty miles back home. You know you are not allowed to drive out of town by yourself. Where were you? Please explain yourself."

Busted, Jenny thought. She knew she could not lie herself out of this situation. *I might as well tell the truth.* "I drove to Bellfield."

Pat paled and sat down quickly on the bed. Jenny was surprised by her mother's reaction to what she had said.

"Are you all right, Mom?"

Pat ignored her question. "Why on earth did you go to Bellfield?"

"I wanted to find out more about Rick Reardon."

"Why?"

"Just curious, I guess."

Pat was so upset, she had to keep her hands in the pockets of her jacket to keep from slapping her daughter. "You are not to go to Bellfield again. Your curiosity about Rick Reardon could cause a lot of problems for many people. You need to forget about him and Bellfield. Do you understand? You are grounded for driving out of town without permission. You cannot drive the car for at least a month. After that time, I will decide when you can use the car again."

Pat was so shaken that she could hardly walk out of the room.

I understand your directive about Bellfield, Jenny thought. *But I will not honor it.*

Jenny wondered how she was going to get through a whole month without a car. She considered asking her friend Marcie to drive her to Bellfield, but she knew that Marcie's mother would not approve the trip. It would not do to have them both without transportation. They might want to attend a movie or a game.

Jenny was anxious to get back to the boutique and speak with the woman she had spoken to during her recent visit there. She was also anxious to get another look at the picture that showed the store's owners. She knew she had never seen these people before. Why did they look so familiar? Why did she feel so shocked when she viewed the picture earlier?

CHAPTER 35

Chuck was encouraged by the easy conversation and relaxed atmosphere that he and Carrie shared at their impromptu dinner meeting two weeks ago, so he decided to see if Carrie would have dinner with him again. He did not have Carrie's phone number, and he did not feel comfortable getting it from the phone company's information line. He was not sure how Carrie would react to that move, so he decided to go to the boutique where she was working.

He was encouraged by the warm smile she gave him when he walked in. "I know you are busy," he told her, "so I will be brief. I have a yen for scallops at the Star Restaurant. Would you like to join me for dinner on Friday night?" He decided not to mention a movie after as he had planned. He did not want to press his luck.

"That would be fine. I will meet you there at six, if that is a good time for you."

"That is great. See you then." Chuck had planned to offer to pick her up and drive her to the restaurant, but something about her demeanor told him not to. *I am really beginning to feel something for that girl*, he thought. *I can't wait for Friday night.*

As Carrie drove to the restaurant, she thought about the things she needed to say to Chuck. She did not want to get into the same situation with Chuck that she had with Pete. *There is no way I am going to tell Chuck, or anyone else for that matter, why I have moved to Bellfield*, she told herself. *However, I do owe him an explanation about myself before we see each other again. He probably will not want to continue our friendship.*

When the waitress saw Chuck and Carrie walk into the restaurant together, she decided to seat them at the special table she reserved for couples she thought would want some privacy. *I don't know why I think that she told herself, but I will seat them at that table anyway.*

When they were seated and had given drink orders, a cocktail for Chuck and coffee for Carrie, Chuck pointed out the fact that they were seated at the same table as before. "Maybe it is some kind of an omen," he said.

Carrie kept the conversation light until she and Chuck were nearly done with their meal.

"Chuck, I need to talk to you."

"Sounds serious."

"It is. Please hear me out." Carrie chose her words carefully as she talked about herself, being sure that Chuck would not be able to relate her story to the reason she was in Bellfield. She told him about living in foster homes until she was eventually placed in the home of Doug and Jane Waters and was brought up by them. She went on to tell him about her aversion to being touched, and finally told him about Pete.

"Have you considered therapy?"

"I went through therapy at Doug and Jane's request when I was in high school. I was not comfortable with the times I spent with the therapist and stopped going to the sessions. Doug and Jane wanted me to continue but respected my decision to stop. They simply asked me to consider resuming therapy at a later time, but I never have."

"Maybe you should."

"Perhaps I will someday." Carrie had decided not to mention to Chuck that she considering counseling with Scott Wynters.

"Carrie, I am not going to let what you just told me interfere with our friendship. I still want to spend time with you. We will just take things slowly and see what develops."

Chuck insisted on paying for both meals when the check arrived. "I invited you out, so as a gentleman I should pay. Maybe we can consider this our first date."

Chuck touched Carrie's arm briefly as he opened her car door for her. He immediately felt her stiffen. *Careful, man, go slow,* he thought.

CHAPTER 36

THE MONDAY AFTER HIS MEETING with Jackie, Scott went to the town's newspaper office. "Good morning, Ed. Would you have newspapers or newspaper articles from approximately twenty years ago?"

Scott would be looking first at the sports pages, so that Ed, or anyone else who might be watching, would not know the subject he was interested in.

"Why on earth is everyone suddenly interested in events that occurred in this town twenty years ago?"

Scott was perplexed. The people from the rehab center Jackie was in would have done their investigation fifteen or twenty years ago. That would not qualify as *suddenly*. "Why? Has someone asked for these papers recently?"

"No, but Jane recently went to lunch with the old ladies' monthly luncheon group." Ed snickered at this comment. "And the ladies there talked about the new gal in town. It seems that she researched newspaper articles at the library and birth records at the town clerk's office from about the same time frame."

And that is exactly why I am here at the newspaper office instead of at the library, Scott told himself. *I hope Ed is not a gossip.* Ed set Scott up in a small room that archived old newspapers. He spent the entire morning reading old newspapers. He read the sport pages first. At the end of the morning, he realized he would not find the information he was looking for in the newspapers. He did not do any better than the people from the rehab center Jackie attended did.

He decided to speak with townspeople who would have been living in Bellfield at the time he was interested in. He decided it would not be wise to speak with Maggie Scranton.

He went to visit John and Maude Abbott. "John?" he asked, "how many years have you been pastor of this church?"

"It will be twenty-five years in June. Why do you ask?"

Scott tried to sound casual. "Oh, I guess curiosity killed the cat. I recently heard an interesting story about a young girl who may have gone missing about twenty years ago. Do you recall hearing any stories about a situation similar to that?"

"I can't say as I do. Maude, do you recall any story like that?"

"Can't say as I do. Scott, why are you so interested?"

"I'm just curious. The person who told me the story could not recall the girl's name. I was wondering if you would know it."

Both John and Maude shook their heads.

"Okay, thanks for your time. By the way, do you remember if there was a family with the last name of Patnode who lived here in Bellfield in about that same time frame?"

Both John and Maude shook their heads again. Scott noticed that John looked agitated.

As soon as Scott and Maude left his office, John picked up the phone. "We may have a serious problem," he said.

CHAPTER 37

CARRIE IMMEDIATELY RECOGNIZED THE ENVELOPE when she went through her mail. *What now?* she thought as she slit the flap open. The familiar block print message said:

> YOU HAVE NOT BEEN HEEDING MY WARNINGS!
> YOU HAVE THIRTY DAYS TO LEAVE TOWN OR SUFFER THE CONSEQUENCES.

"What if I don't leave town? What are the consequences? What will you do?" she asked the letter as she held it in her hand. She decided to make two calls. The first was to Scott Wynters. "Scott, this is Carrie Franklin. Did Nan show you the strange letters I have received lately?"

"Yes, she did and I have read them. They concern me a great deal. It is obvious that someone, probably someone who lives in this town, is threatened by your presence here."

"How can that be? I have only lived here a few months. I have not had any contact with anyone in town except the people I work with and the people I have met at the church socials."

"You told Nan that you think you may possibly have roots here in Bellfield. If you do, these letters might have something to do with your life as a very young child, something you may not be able to recall because of your young age. Are you comfortable coming in to talk with me about this matter?"

"Yes, I think I am now ready to talk with you."

"Can you come in next Tuesday after work?"

"Yes, I can. You can update me on how Nan is doing these days."

"I can do that now. Except for her being a little uncomfortable carrying all the extra weight, she is doing fine. By the way, I want you to know how much I appreciate your concern for Nan's well-being. You made the right decision not to continue having contact with her until we figure out just who is harassing you. We do not know if this person is a danger, or just someone with a misguided agenda."

"I just did not want to put Nan in a precarious situation. See you Tuesday."

What an interesting week I have coming up, Scott thought as he hung up the phone.

Carrie's next call was to her parents.

"How wonderful to hear from you," Jane said when she heard Carrie's voice on the line. "Your dad and I were just talking about visiting you next weekend if that works for you."

"I would love to see you, but I have something to tell you that cannot wait that long."

"Is everything okay?" Jane asked nervously.

"I don't know. One thing I need to tell you is that I am going to start seeing a therapist."

"That is great news, Carrie."

"You may not feel that way when you find out the reason that I am seeing the therapist." Carrie proceeded to tell Jane about the letters she has received. "So you see, I am not just seeing this person for therapy. I also need to talk with someone I trust about what to do with these letters."

"Do you trust this Scott Wynters?"

"I don't really know him well, but I have developed a strong friendship with his wife, Nan, and I trust her completely. I gave her the first two letters I received for Scott to read. She told me he would keep them safe in his office safe, and he did that."

"Your dad will want to see them."

"I will get them on Tuesday when I see Scott in his office. I made the decision not to continue to have lunch with Nan until the mystery of the letters is cleared up. She is expecting a baby boy soon, and I don't want anything to upset her."

"That is typical of you, Carrie. Always being concerned for other people. See you next weekend."

Carrie had decided not to mention Chuck to her mother.

CHAPTER 38

RICK WAS VERY IRRITATED WHEN the phone rang. He was busy writing up orders for new merchandise and did not want to be disturbed.

"Unique Boutique, may I help you?"

"I would like to speak with the owner of this business."

"There are two owners, Rick and Nancy Reardon. This is Rick Reardon."

"Listen carefully. My daughter, your daughter, came across a twenty-year-old newspaper article about you that I thought was well hidden. I did not have a good explanation as to why I saved the article. This made her curious about you, so she went to your boutique, hoping to learn more about what was written in the article. Thankfully, you were not at the boutique when she was there. The person who was working at the boutique refused to give her any information. I have forbidden her to go to Bellfield again, but she is very stubborn and may not obey me. If she does return there, you must see to it that she does not learn about our relationship." The phone clicked.

Can anything else go wrong? Rick thought when he learned that Jackie had not shown up for work. The only bright spot of this day was that Nancy was not in the office when the call came in. He was so shocked by the voice on the other end of the line that he was not sure that he could correctly recall all that was said. *At least I don't have to explain anything to Nancy*, he said to himself.

"Have you tried to call Jackie to see if she is ill?" he asked Nancy when she returned to the boutique.

"No, maybe she just overslept. Let's give her a few more minutes, and I will call her. I don't want her to think we are upset with her the first time she is late."

Carrie heard the conversation. "This is not like Jackie. She is very committed to her work here. I am a little worried."

"Don't worry," Nancy answered. "We will get to the bottom of this soon."

Nancy made several calls to Jackie but received no response. "I am going to drive over to her apartment and see if she is okay," Nancy told Rick.

Within a half hour, Nancy was back to the store. "I knocked on the door and rang the bell several times, but received no response," she told Rick and Carrie. "I think I will call the police and ask them to do a wellness check."

Sgt. Paul Tennyson answered the call. "Bellfield Police Department, can I help you?"

"This is Nancy Reardon from the Unique Boutique. I am concerned about an employee of ours. Her name is Jackie Patnode. She did not show up for work today, which has never happened before. I have phoned her several times this morning, but she has not answered her phone. I went to her apartment. Her doors were all locked. I rang the bell several times, pounded on the door, and called her name. I did not receive a response. I am a little worried. Can you do a wellness check?" Nancy gave him Jackie's phone number and address.

"I will see what I can find out about her and get back to you."

Paul called Jackie several times, but like Nancy she did not receive an answer. He drove to Jackie's apartment complex and noted how well cared for everything looked. *I am sure there is not a problem here,* he thought, *but I had better talk with the apartment manager and see what I can find out.*

Bruce Tucker was surprised to find a policeman at his door.

"Is there a problem, Officer?" he asked

"Probably not. What can you tell me about the occupant of apartment 7?"

"Her name is Jackie Patnode. She is very quiet, lives alone, and seldom goes out except to work. She always pays her rent on time."

"Does she have many visitors?"

"Almost never."

"She did not show up for work today and does not answer her phone. Her employer came to the apartment, but she did not answer the door. The employer is pretty worried. I think I better check the apartment to see if she is okay. She may be ill."

Paul knocked on the door and called Jackie's name several times before he used the key the apartment manager had given him and let himself in. He immediately noted how well kept and neat the apartment was. He carefully searched the four rooms in the apartment and called out Jackie's name as he did so. He was certain that no one was in the apartment. He noticed that the bed in the bedroom was unmade and rumpled, which was incongruous to everything else he had observed in the home. He decided to report this to the chief before contacting Jackie's employers.

As he was leaving the apartment, he noticed a picture of Jackie and the Reardons that was clipped from the newspaper. The article stated that Jackie had been hired as a consultant to the shop's clientele. *You can tell the boutique is a classy place,* he thought. Other shops would consider her a clerk, and the people who'd come into the store customers.

He looked at the picture again. *I think I have seen this woman before. I wonder where.*

CHAPTER 39

Carrie was exhausted Tuesday evening when it was time to leave work and drive to Scott's office for her appointment. She had had to do Jackie's work and deal with her own feelings about Jackie's disappearance, and another event of the day.

The Reardons were of no help. They had remained somewhat stoic when Sgt. Tennyson came to the store and told him that he, like Nancy, was unable to reach her by phone. He went on to tell them about going to her apartment. He explained how neat and tidy the apartment was, suggesting that nothing unusual had happened there. He and Chief Jacobs had decided not to mention the unmade, rumpled bed he had seen.

"We will continue searching for Ms. Patnode," he told the Reardons. "I am returning to her apartment now to do a more thorough search, to search her car, go through her financial records. I could not do that before because I did not have a warrant."

As soon as Sgt. Tennyson left the store, the Reardons shut themselves up in their office. Carrie could see them through the office windows and could tell they were having an animated conversation. *I would like to be a fly on that wall,* Carrie thought.

Carrie had something else to contemplate as she drove on. Chuck had come into the store at a time that she was her busiest. "I'll be brief," he said. "How about Italian on Saturday night? I'll drive. The place I am thinking about is a little way out of town and difficult to find."

"My parents are visiting me this weekend."

"Do they like Italian?"

"They do."

"Great. I will pick the three of you up at your apartment around six thirty."

At that moment, a customer asked Carrie's opinion of a handbag she was considering purchasing. "See you then," Carrie said, without thinking the response through.

I hope I did not make a mistake about Saturday night, Carrie thought as she parked in the lot outside Scott's office.

Scott greeted Carrie the same way he had greeted Jackie the night before. He hung up her coat for her and offered coffee.

"Coffee sounds great. It has been a trying day."

"You do look a little tired," Scott responded.

Carrie thought it would be all right to tell Scott about Jackie not showing up for work, and about Nancy and Sgt. Tennyson's failed attempts to reach her.

Scott was shaken. He was glad that Carrie had accepted his offer of coffee. It gave him a minute to make a phone call. "Paul," he said, when his call was answered, "how long are you going to be at the precinct?"

"Great," he responded, when his question was answered. "I have a client that will be here for about an hour, then I will be over to share some information that I think you will find interesting.

He did not mention that the information concerned Jackie Patnode.

Scott returned with Carrie's coffee and sat down behind his desk. "Do you want to talk or it too stressful a time for you?"

"I am here. I will stay and talk for a while. What has Nan told you about me?"

"Very little. We both knew you were a potential client. I can't discuss my clients with Nan or anyone else because of confidentially. She has told me that she considers you to be a very nice, intelligent young girl whose past has caused you a great deal of stress. She did tell me that you are here in town to find your roots. I hope I can help you with that."

"I don't recall anything about my life until I was about five years of age."

"That is not that unusual. Some children may recall a little about their life when they are about four years old. Most cannot recall any earlier part of their lives. You are not that far off the mark."

"I don't know anything about my parents. I assume I had some." Carried chuckled. "My first recollection is of being in a foster home. I was moved sound a lot because I was a very difficult child. I would not have been so difficult if people had just left me alone."

"How so?"

Carrie went on to tell Scott what she could recall about her life before being placed with Jane and Doug Waters. "There was always a lot of other children in the home. They demanded that I play with those children, when all I wanted was to be by myself. When they put me to bed at night, they tried to give me a hug or a goodnight kiss. They didn't really care about me. They just tried to do what the books said they had to be good foster parents. I retaliated by refusing to eat, refusing to become toilet trained, and refusing to attend preschool.

"When I went to live with Doug and Jane, they did not make those demands on me. The first few months that I lived there, there was one other child in the household, a little boy. Doug and Jane allowed each of us to play by ourselves. We did not share the same interests and did not enjoy playing with the same toys.

"The only time that Doug and Jane made me connect physically with them was when they had to hold my hand when in crowds, crossing streets. I hated the physical contact, but understood it was for safety reasons, therefore endured it."

Carrie went on to tell Scott about her years in school, her work with the therapist, and about Pete.

"Carrie, has anyone ever explained the term *reactive attachment disorder* to you?"

"Yes, my therapist and Doug and Jane."

"The first thing I noticed about you when I saw you at the church social was the clever ways you have developed to avoid physical contact. The acronym RAD immediately came to my mind as I watched you. I assume something traumatic happened to you when you were a very young child. We need to discover what that was."

"How?"

"Hypnosis may help."

"I am not ready for that."

"Then we won't do it until you are ready. I have another suggestion. You need to try to allow someone close to you to briefly touch you. You could tolerate hand-holding when you were young because you understood that it was necessary. Well, this is necessary also. I assume that the problem with Pete was that he wanted too much too fast. Try a brief, small physical contact with someone you love and trust, someone who understands you, probably your foster parents."

"My parents are coming to visit me this weekend."

"Great! Do they know you are seeing me?"

"Yes, I told Jane over the phone the last time I spoke with her."

"Then see if you can try this little bit of therapy. Just one time would be a step in the right direction."

Carrie decided to tell Scott about Chuck. "My parents and I are going to dinner at a small Italian restaurant Saturday evening with Chuck Warner."

"That is good news. I think Chuck is seriously interested in developing a relationship with you. All the more reason for you to start the touch therapy."

"I told my parents about the threatening letters I have been receiving. My dad wants to see them."

"I will get them from my safe."

Boy, do I wish I could talk with Chuck about Carrie, Scott told himself after Carrie left his office.

Scott called Nan to tell her would be a little later getting home. "No problem," she said. "I will hold dinner."

She is the perfect wife for me, Scott told himself. *She never complains when I am later getting home.*

I am glad I made copies of these letters, Scott thought as he put on his jacket. *I hope what I am about to do is not too unethical.*

After emptying his pockets and going through the screening process, Scott went directly to Paul Tennyson's office. "I understand that Jackie Patnode is missing," he said to Paul.

"I cannot comment on that," Paul replied. "The information has not gone out to the public as yet."

"And I cannot divulge how I came by the information I am going to share with you. And I am probably doing something I shouldn't be doing." He placed the copies of Jackie's and Carrie's letters on Paul's desk and left without another word.

Paul read the letters. *These are similar letters to two women who have absolutely no connection with each other than that they work for the same employer,* he mused. *Is there a connection, or is it just a coincidence? I don't believe in coincidences.* Several thoughts flickered through Paul's mind, but they did not connect to his brain.

CHAPTER 40

Carrie was excited to see Doug and Jane drive up Maggie's driveway. They had called her and told her they were in town and would be at her apartment as soon as they checked into the Motel 6, so she was watching for them. She was happy she had told Jane about the letters. She wanted to show them to her dad and get his advice about how to handle the situation. All this was too heavy a burden for her to carry alone.

Doug and Jane both wished they could hug Carrie when they entered her apartment, but they knew they could not.

"I thought you might be hungry after your drive, and we won't be having dinner for a while, so I made coffee to go with some cookies I bought at the local bakery. I don't know if you have noticed it, but there is a small bakery in the same mall where the Motel 6 and the Star Restaurant are located. Its pastries are all homemade and are delicious. The Star is the restaurant we had dinner at the last time you were here. Sit down at the table, and I will pour the coffee and set out the cookies. Then we can talk."

"Where do you want to have dinner tonight?" Doug asked. "The Star Restaurant has a varied menu, so I don't mind going back there. I assume Bellfield doesn't have many dining choices."

"Actually, plans for tonight's dinner have already been made. We have reservations at an Italian restaurant a little way out of town. I don't know exactly where it is."

"Then how are we supposed to get there?" Doug questioned.

"We are going with a friend of mine. His name is Chuck Warner, and he is going to pick us up here at the apartment. He and I have had dinner together at the Star a couple of times. The first time, we met there accidentally. The second time, we planned to meet there."

Doug and Jane exchanged glances. Doug shook his head, slightly telling Jane not to mention Charles Warner.

Carrie noticed the exchanged glances and misread them. "Right now, we are just friends," she explained. Chuck understands I am not ready for a serious relationship." She wondered why she had said right now.

"Before we go to dinner, I will show you the letters I have been receiving, but there is something else I want to talk about. Dad, do you remember when I was little, you and Mom insisted that one of you had to hold my hand when we were in crowds or when we were crossing the street?"

"I do. You were determined that it be your mother that held your hand. You seemed to be afraid of being touched by men."

"Scott Wynters, my therapist, believes that I was able to tolerate that physical contact because I understood it was important. He wants me to understand that any physical contact is important. He wants me to allow Jane or someone to touch me briefly. He wants me to experience being touched as often and as long as I can tolerate it. He believes that, with time, I will lose my aversion to being touched. He also wants to delve into my past to find out what happened to me as a very young child to cause this aversion. He wants to use hypnosis. That frightens me, and I am not ready for that yet."

"When does he want you to begin this strategy?"

"As soon as I feel comfortable doing it."

"Are you comfortable now?"

"We can try."

Jane walked over to Carrie and placed her hand gently on her shoulder. Carrie shuddered, allowed the contact briefly, then moved away.

Doug wanted to ease the tension he saw in Carrie's demeanor. "Now that we have that done, let's take a look at the letters you have been receiving."

Carrie removed the letters from her purse and handed them to Doug. He read them carefully, then handed them to Jane to read.

"How many townspeople know the real reason for your move to Bellfield?"

"Only Nan and Scott, and they didn't know until after I received the second letter."

"How many people know that you went to the library and town office to search for your 'cousin'?"

"Probably the whole town. People here gossip constantly. Everyone knows everyone's business."

"Have you visited the cemetery?"

"Yes."

"Who would know about that visit?"

"I don't know. Anyone could have seen me. I tried to make my visit appear like a casual walk for exercise, but anyone could have observed the fact that I stopped and read names on the monuments that were there. I need to tell you about a house I visited on Brook Street."

Carrie went on to tell Doug and Jane about encountering the house on Brook Street when she located the houses with the addresses that she found at the town clerk's office, and about her subsequent visits.

"No one would be aware of those visits, would they?" Jane asked.

"Oh yes, they would." Carrie told them about the conversations held at the dinner party at the Warners' home.

"Why were you visiting the Warners?" Jane did not like what she was hearing.

"I was invited to a dinner party. I went with my landlady, Maggie Scranton."

"Carrie," Doug said, "we need to take these letters very seriously. Apparently, someone feels threatened by your presence in Bellfield, by your research, and by your visits to the cemetery and the house on Brook Street. You may be in danger. I think you should pack up and come home with us."

"I can't do that. I think the answers to my past are in this town. I want to find those answers."

"Then we need to take these letters to the police. Maybe they will be willing to keep an eye on you. Let's head over to the police department right now."

CHAPTER 41

After reading the letters both Jackie and Carrie had received, Sgt. Paul Tennyson perused old and current police and town records to see if he could find a link between Jackie Patnode and Carrie Franklin. He was shocked to find no evidence that either woman had lived in Bellfield in the past. Carrie had arrived in town about four months ago. Jackie had come to Bellfield many years ago to work at the Unique Boutique. Her history before that time was a complete mystery.

He contemplated interviewing the Reardons to see if they could shed light on Jackie's past. He would have to be careful not to mention anything about the letters. As far as he knew, no one except the Wynters and Jackie and Carrie themselves knew about the letters, and he needed to keep it that way. *Of course, the person who wrote the letters also knows about them*, he thought sardonically.

Before Paul was able to get out of the office to go and speak with the Reardons, he saw three people come into the station. Paul recognized Carrie, the new person in town who was receiving the letters. Doug walked up to Paul's desk and introduced himself, Jane, and Carrie. "We are here," he explained, "because my daughter, Carrie, has been receiving letters with veiled threats. I would like to have you read them, and see what you think should be done about them. I am worried about Carrie's safety."

Paul read the letters carefully. He did not want Carrie or the Waters to know he had seen them before. *The fewer people who know about my involvement with this case, the better*, he thought.

"Haven't you been in town for just a few months?" he asked Carrie.

"Yes, about four months." Paul already knew that answer.

"Have you ever lived here previously?"

"I don't know, maybe."

Paul was confused by that answer. "Either you did or you didn't."

"Carrie's background is nebulous at best," Doug explained. "She came to live in our town, which is about an hour's drive from here, when she was about four years old. No one knew, or if they knew were not saying, where she came from. There were some indications that she was from Bellfield."

Carrie spoke up. "I came here to find out if I had lived here as a very young child, but I don't want that fact to be widely known."

"How old are you?"

"I am twenty-one."

Dear god, Paul thought. *Could she be that little girl? Does the person who abused her suspect who she is? If that person is suspicious of that fact, Carrie might be in real danger. Would she be able to recall what had happened to her? Would she recognize her abuser?* He doubted it. She was too young.

Doug waited patiently while Paul processed this information. "I think," Paul stated, "that someone must know about your past, if indeed you do have a history here."

"What led you to believe Carrie is from Bellfield?" Paul asked Doug and Jane.

"There was a phone number attached to her brief records. The exchange is Bellfield's."

"Do you have that phone number?"

"I do not. The agency that placed Carrie into foster care may have that number."

"All information about Carrie was always very hush-hush. To be honest, I think someone in very high places knows Carrie's past and wants to keep it quiet."

Paul knew that was not true if Carrie was the child Maggie Scranton rescued from the steps of the house on Brook Street all those years ago. There had been no way to identify either the child or the woman found in the same building. Paul and Nell Warner had decided to keep all information about Carrie's secret for her own protection. Their tactic had obviously worked very well.

"I need to keep these letters," Paul told Carrie. "I will give you copies if you like."

"I don't need copies. I will never forget what those letters said."

"I would like copies," Doug stated.

Jane, who had mostly remained quiet during this time, spoke up. "I am worried about my daughter's safety. We want her to come back home with us, but she prefers to stay here."

"Where do you live, Carrie?"

Paul was surprised when he learned that Carrie was renting Maggie Scranton's garage apartment. *I am sure Maggie has no idea who this girl may be, but still it is not a good situation,* he thought.

"I can check in with you from time to time to be sure everything is okay, but I can't do much more than that. Maybe you should heed your parents' advice and go home with them for a while."

"No, I am going to stay here and see this through. Is there any way you can find out where the letters came from?"

"I will try. They were probably mailed from a corner mailbox on some street here in town. That would make it difficult to find out who dropped them off."

"What about forensics?" Doug suggested.

"I will see what I can do, but this is a small department with few resources. Give me some time. I will see what I can find out."

After getting the copies of the letters, Doug, Jane, and Carrie left the building. Neither Doug nor Jane was satisfied with their meeting at the police department.

CHAPTER 42

Doug and Jane enjoyed the ride to the Italian restaurant. It was a lovely evening, and the scenery was beautiful. Doug was invited to sit in the front seat of the car with Chuck, with the two women sitting in the back, but he declined the offer. He insisted that Carrie ride in the front with Chuck, with him and Jane in the back. He wanted to observe the body language between Chuck and Carrie. He could see Carrie hold herself stiff; Chuck was a perfect gentleman.

Conversation between the four adults flowed easily throughout most of the dinner until Jane asked about Chuck's father. Doug shot her a look of disapproval, but it was too late.

"I think I might have gone to school with your father, she said. I saw you with your parents at the Star Restaurant a couple weeks ago, and I think I may have recognized him. Did he attend UVM?"

Chuck tensed but answered in an even manner. "He did, then continued on to Harvard Law School. After he passed his bar exam, he settled back here to start his law practice. He and Mom had dated in high school, but their relationship did not get serious until after he started his practice. She applied for the job of secretary to his firm, and he hired her. The rest is history. Why do you ask?"

"No reason. I just wondered if he was the same Charles Warner I knew at school. I am happy to see that he is doing so well."

Chuck was sure that Jane was aware of his father's history at UVM. He was glad she did not bring it up. He wondered if she had told the story to Carrie. *It doesn't matter*, he thought. *If this relationship goes anywhere, I will tell her myself. There should be no secrets in a serious relationship.*

Doug wanted to change the subject. "I understand you work in your dad's law firm."

"Yes, I did the same as my dad. After graduating high school, I went to UVM then to Harvard. After I passed the bar, I applied for positions in law firms in New York, New Jersey, and the city of Chicago. I had several interviews and even got some offers. I considered the offers, checked out apartments, etc. But soon I realized that I did not belong in big cities. I am like my parents. I am a country boy at heart."

"So you rejected these offers and returned to Vermont?"

"I did. I like the mountains and the rural atmosphere. I have great memories of visiting the park on the west side of town with my parents. I remember the swings, the seesaws, the sandboxes. If, or I guess when, I marry and raise a family I want my children to experience the kind of life that I have experienced. I would not want to raise children in a big city."

As Chuck was talking, tears began to roll down Carrie's cheeks. "I think I may have experienced some of those things," she said in a barely audible whisper.

CHAPTER 43

At first, Jackie thought she was having the dream again. But something was different; something was wrong. She felt ill and confused like in her dream, but she was not in her bed. When she begged not to have the shot again, she did not wake up; instead she got the shot.

I cannot remember what happened after she left the mall. How long ago was that? A day, a week, longer? Who is the man in the mask who is continually administering the shots? He wore a mask, but there was something familiar about him. Who is he? Why is he doing this?

Soon after leaving Jackie, he received a call from the bank. He was relieved to learn that the closing on the property had been completed. He had asked the manager of his "corporation" to have the closing moved up by two weeks, and this request had obviously been honored. He could not risk having anyone go into the house. Now that he officially owned the property, he could properly secure it.

He was not the only one happy to have the closing completed. Both Ben and Barb Barker and the bank manager were happy to have this albatross removed from their necks.

Barb Barker spoke to Ben as they left the bank after signing the required papers. "Something is not right," she told her husband. "I question why all the secrecy over a property with so little value. I hope we are not involved with something illegal or nefarious."

"*Nefarious* is a very strong term, Barb. I wonder why you chose to use that word."

"I wonder too. It just popped into my head. I hope it is not an omen of something that is about to happen." Barb had no idea what she was purporting.

The bank manager observed the Barkers exit the bank. *I wonder if they are as uncomfortable with this transaction as I am*, he mused.

He watched the Barkers walk out of the bank, and could see the manager looking at them out the window. *I need to be careful*, he told himself. They might have some reservations about the closing transaction. I think I am covered. The taxes and insurance will be taken care of by the corporation. I hope there will not be any emergency expenses, but if there are the corporation will cover them also.

CHAPTER 44

"We need to get our stories straight before Paul Tennyson gets here," Rick told Nancy.

"Sgt. Paul Tennyson," Nancy reminded Rick. "He wants to learn what we know about Jackie's background."

"Which is nothing."

"Really." Nancy smirked.

Rick flinched. "We must tell him, again, that we know nothing about her. She came in and asked for work. She was totally honest, stating that she had no references because she had not worked for a while. She said she had been ill, but she did not elaborate. Because she was honest and straightforward, and because we had been having a difficult time filling the position, we hired her on the spot."

"With your reputation, he will not have trouble believing that."

Rick ignored the comment. "Where do you think Jackie is?"

"I don't know, but I don't think she left on her own volition. We know John forced you to hire Jackie in exchange for keeping quiet about your little affair. He went so far as to relocate the girl and her family using church funds to save the reputation of the church. If anyone found out that he did that, John would be in deep trouble. Perhaps someone did find this out and decided to 'relocate' Jackie."

"That was nearly twenty years ago. Why do something now? Nothing has changed to upset the balance of the church or the town."

"Oh really? Don't we have a new girl in town researching the past?"

"Carrie? There can't be any connection."

"I know that since Carrie has come to town there has been a lot of speculation about why she is here and what she is really searching for. I know that since Carrie has worked here, Jackie has become distracted and nervous, and has now disappeared. I know that Pat Lawrence's daughter has visited this town and that Pat called and threatened you."

Rick gasped. "How did you find that out?"

"I checked the phone tapes while searching for some buyer's prices I had lost and came across the call. All this has to be more than just happenstance."

Before Rick could reply, Paul Tennyson came into the shop. Carrie was surprised to see him there so soon after she and her parents had met with him at the police station.

"Hello, sergeant, what can I do for you?"

"I am here to see the Reardons."

Just then, Rick came out of the office to meet Paul. "Carrie," he said, "Nancy and I are going to meet with Sgt. Tennyson in the office for a few minutes. Can you handle things out here?"

"I can."

"If you need anything, tap on the door, and one of us will be out to assist you."

"I will be fine."

As soon as the three of them had settled in the office, Paul got right to the point. "I want you to tell me everything you know about Jackie Patnode."

"We told you everything we know when we spoke the last time." Rick went on to repeat the same story he and Nancy had agreed on earlier.

Without making a comment on what Rick had just said, Paul turned to Nancy. "Tell me what you know about Jackie's past."

"All I know is what Rick just told you."

"I find your story hard to believe. We are dealing with the mysterious disappearance of a woman who has worked for you for several years. I am convinced that you know something that you refuse to reveal. I am suspicious of the fact that you show so little concern for a longtime employee. If you know something that you are not telling me, I will see to it that there are repercussions for you acts."

Paul abruptly left the store.

CHAPTER 45

PAUL HAD A RULE AGAINST discussing his police work with anyone outside his department. He didn't even discuss his cases with his wife. However, right now, he was giving serious consideration to breaking this rule. He desperately needed to find more information about Jackie Patnode. He had called rehab centers within a fifty-mile radius of Bellfield but learned nothing new. He was told they could not answer questions about a patient, and could not confirm or deny if a person by the name of Jackie Patnode received treatment at their facility. They cited privacy laws.

Against his better judgement, Paul decided to talk with Maggie Scranton. She had lived in Bellfield for over fifty years and was active in town affairs. If anyone in town knew anything about Jackie's background, it would be Maggie.

When Paul arrived at Maggie's house, she offered coffee and cookies, which he declined.

Maggie made it easy for Paul to broach the subject of Jackie. She brought it up herself.

"Paul," Maggie said, "there are some strange things happening in Bellfield right now that really worry me."

"What kinds of things?"

"Things that involve our two most mysterious residents."

"And who might that be?"

"Paul, I am not stupid. You know who I am talking about. The two who arrived in town under mysterious circumstances: Jackie Patnode and my tenant, Carrie Franklin. Carrie is a sweet girl, but there is something strange going on with her."

"Let's talk about Jackie Patnode. Why do you think her coming to Bellfield is strange?"

"She just showed up in town one day and immediately got a job. She also had an apartment ready for her as well as a car. If that is not strange, I don' know what is."

"Where does she say she lived before coming here?" Paul asked hopefully.

"She doesn't say. She refuses to discuss her past."

Another dead end. Paul groaned to himself.

"And now," Maggie went on, "Jackie seems to have disappeared."

Paul was surprised that Maggie had that information. "Why do you say that?"

"Because Jane Croteau has been to the Unique Boutique and asked for her. The Reardons simply say that Jackie will be out for a few days. They will not say where she is or when she will return to work."

Paul was glad to know that Rick and Nancy were both honoring his request not to tell anyone about Jackie's disappearance. He realized that he would not learn anything more from Maggie about Jackie.

"What about Carrie Franklin?"

"She is a sweet girl and a perfect tenant, but no one believes she is here to look for a lost cousin. She did research at the library and town clerk's office when she first got here, but she has not done any since. She has some strange behaviors. She wanders around the cemetery and stands in front of that old abandoned house on Brook Street, shaking. I think she is afraid of that house for some reason. When she first moved into the garage apartment, she asked me if there was a way to get here without passing the house. I thought that was a strange question. Lately, she seems nervous about getting her mail. Sometimes when I separate her mail from mine, I see a strange envelope with no return address. I think that mail, whatever it is, makes her nervous."

Paul did not get the information he wanted about Jackie, but was excited about what Maggie had said about Carrie and the house on Brook Street. He was anxious to get back to his office to do some research and make a phone call.

"Maggie, thank you for the nice chat. I need to get back to my office to attend a meeting."

After Paul left, Maggie suddenly realized that she had no idea why Paul had come to visit her.

CHAPTER 46

As much as Paul wanted to pursue the case of the little girl found many years ago at the house on Brook Street, he knew that his first priority was to search for Jackie Patnode. He had no idea if she was in imminent danger, or if she had just decided to leave town without telling anyone where she would be staying. The later, however, did not seem plausible. If she had decided to relocate, why had she left all her possessions at the apartment?

Paul spent the morning searching for information regarding Jackie. He located current information, such as her bank account, but was surprised to learn that there did not seem to be any information about her before she moved to Bellfield. There was no social security information, no bank account, credit cards, no former addresses or phone numbers, nothing.

He called the social security office and learned they had not issued her a social security card. The person he spoke with would not give him her social security number but did research her name. "The number she has seems to be appropriate," he was told. Paul next called the Internal Revenue Service office in Connecticut where Vermont tax returns are filed. Both Paul and the agent he was speaking with were surprised to learn that no one named Jackie Patnode ever paid income taxes until Jackie started to work at the Unique Boutique, yet her date of birth indicated that Jackie was forty-one years old. She may not have earned income before this time, but she should have been given a social security number at birth. "Something strange is going on here," the agent stated.

Tell me about it, Paul thought.

Paul then went to the town clerk's office and asked to see birth records for the mid-1970s. "These birth records seem to have become popular reading material lately," Nora Ryan remarked. Paul did not comment, but he went straight to the selectman's office and started reading.

Paul hoped his frustration at finding no information about Jackie did not show as he handed the records back to Nora and left the town clerk's office. *My next stop will be the church,* he thought. *Maybe there will be some baptismal records that will help.* He had no idea what a mistake that move would be.

I will have something interesting to tell the ladies at our next luncheon, Nora thought.

CHAPTER 47

Nell Warner was surprised that her caller ID indicated that her call was from the Bellfield Police Department. She decided to answer the call formally. "This is Nell Warner."

"Nell, this is Sgt. Paul Tennyson from the Bellfield Police Department. I am calling to see if you would have time to meet me for coffee sometime soon. I would like to discuss one of your earlier cases."

"Paul, I am retired."

"I know that, but this is very important. I won't take up a lot of your time, and I think this is something that would be okay for you to discuss with me."

"When do you want to meet?"

"Give me a couple of days to do some research, then I will get back to you."

"I won't promise I will give you any information about any of my cases, but I am willing to meet with you and hear you out."

"Great. I will get back to you in a couple of days."

That is a start, Paul thought. *I wouldn't be able to get anywhere without Nell's help.*

Paul's next call was to the office of Dr. Patrick Adams. He identified himself. "I need to speak with the doctor about a child he examined several years ago," he told the receptionist. "Is there a time I could meet with him? I would not need more than a few minutes."

"Dr. Adams does have a break in his schedule because of a cancellation. How soon could you be here?"

"In about five minutes."

When Paul was greeted by Dr. Adams, he was surprised to see how little the doctor had changed in eighteen years. He had a few laugh lines, but other than that, he had aged very little. His handshake was firm and his demeanor professional. *Good,* Paul thought, *he should be a good resource for my research.*

Paul was hoping he could get the information that he was seeking from the doctor without mentioning Carrie. "Would you still have a record of a child you examined at the hospital several years ago?" Paul gave the doctor the date that he and Nell had brought the child Maggie had found to the hospital.

Dr. Adams was apparently very organized. His file cabinets were labeled by decades, and he was able to quickly pull the file Paul requested.

"I only saw this child the one time. It was a very sad situation. The child was a girl about three, or three and a half years old. It appeared to me that she had been a victim of attempted sexual assault.

"The attempt to penetrate was not completed. She did not seem to be injured otherwise. There was no sign of broken bones. She did, however, have several bruises that suggested that she was handled roughly. The child would or could not speak. She would or could not tell her name, where she lived, or anything about her parents. She was not able to interact with anyone, not even the nurse assigned to care for her. That nurse had been handpicked for that duty because she was a warm, loving person. I know it was necessary for you and the social worker with you to place the child in the care of family services. We released her to the services when she no longer required hospital care. I was present when she left the hospital. She did not react to her situation at all. She just seemed to be resigned to anything that might happen to her. It was such a sad situation that tears stung my eyes."

Paul was moved by the empathy that Dr. Adams had shown for the child. He had taken careful notes of their conversation. "I may have to return with a court order to get copies of your files. With a court order, I will be happy to release the files to you. Why the sudden interest in this case? Did you ever discover who injured that little girl, or find out what happened to her after she left the hospital?"

"That is what I am trying to find out."

Paul thanked the doctor and left the office even more determined to solve this cold case.

CHAPTER 48

CARRIE WAS MORE RELAXED THE second time she visited Scott's office. He had a friendly, professional manner and did not pressure her into talking until she was ready. She wanted to talk to Scott about her feelings about Jackie. She could not explain to herself why she was feeling such a loss over Jackie's disappearance. *I've only known her for a few months,* she thought. She also wanted to tell Scott about the events of the weekend of her parents' visit.

Scott brought Carrie a cup of coffee and suggested she take a few minutes to unwind before they'd start talking. Carrie was soon ready to talk. She told Scott about the dinner with Chuck and how everyone seemed to enjoy each other's company. Scott tried to maintain a sense of calm when she told him about her flicks of recall when Chuck talked about going to the playground with his parents, and about the sandbox and swings. He certainly intended to pursue these memories with Carrie when he thought Carrie was ready to take that step.

She went on to tell Scott about taking her intimidating letters to Sgt. Tennyson at the police department, and how he had taken the content of the letters very seriously. Scott was glad the letters went to the sergeant. *He and I are the only ones who know that two women are receiving threatening letters. If there is a connection to these two events, Sgt. Tennyson will find it,* he assured himself.

"Scott," Carrie said in an excited voice. "I have saved the best of the weekend for last. I tried the touch therapy that you suggested with my mom. I allowed her to touch me, but only very briefly, and I think I will be able to do it again. Enduring the touch was easier than I thought it would be. Probably because it was Jane who did it. My parents will be down again in a couple of weeks, and I will try the experiment again."

Carrie continued with the next thing on her mind. She told him about her intense feelings about Jackie's disappearance. "I don't know why I feel such a loss," Carrie said. "I have only known Jackie for a few months. We work together and occasionally have lunch together, but that is all there is to our relationship."

"You are a kind, caring person," Scott told Carrie. "I don't think your feelings are unusual."

To himself, Scott thought. *I am beginning to sense some sort of connection between these two that, currently, no one understands. I wish I could speak to Paul Tennyson about this matter,* Scott told himself. *But of course, I cannot.*

When Carrie left the office, Carrie and Scott both thought the session had been very helpful.

She's really been talking up a storm, Scott thought. Nothing could be better.

CHAPTER 49

Maude was surprised when Sgt. Tennyson arrived at her door. She wondered what a member of the Bellfield Police Department would want at the church rectory. At Paul's request Maude ushered him into John's office. She wanted to stay to see what Sgt. Tennyson would say, but the look John gave her told her that she had to leave the room.

"What can I do for you?" John asked Paul.

"Do you keep records of all church baptisms?"

"All baptisms are recorded in the church Bible, and certificates of baptism are given to the parents. I have copies of all the certificates."

"Can I see the copies of certificates presented in the mid-1970s?"

"Sure. They are public record. You can also find records of births in the town clerk's office."

"I have been there. I could not locate the information I was seeking."

John knew better than to ask Paul what information he was searching for. He brought the requested baptismal records and the church Bible to Paul. "I have to attend a meeting," he told Paul. "You can use the desk in my study to do your research. Just leave everything there on the desk when you are finished."

Paul spent nearly two hours reading through the certificates and all the entries in the Bible from the time he was interested in. He had lived in Bellfield all his life and knew most of the people whose names were recorded in the Bible and on the certificates. He found nothing at all that could relate to Carrie Franklin and Jackie Patnode. Discouraged, he left the information on John's desk, calling goodbye to Maude, and then he left the rectory.

As soon as Paul was out of the driveway, Maude rushed into John's office to see what Paul was doing there. She saw the Bible and baptismal certificates and surmised what Paul was interested in.

Maude hated going against her husband, but she had to protect him. She made the necessary call.

CHAPTER 50

Charles Warner knew that his son, Chuck, was falling in love with Carrie Franklin. He had no idea if the feeling was reciprocated. He was worried about this situation and decided to do some internet searching to see if he could learn more about Carrie. He had learned from Chuck that Carrie's foster parents lived in Norwich, Vermont, so he started his search there. He searched school and hospital records, but found nothing before Carrie went to live with the Waters. After over an hour's search, Charles came to the conclusion that there was no history of Carrie before she reached the age of four. *What the heck is going on?* he wondered.

At that time, Chuck walked into the room. "Are you working on the King case?" he asked his father.

"No, I am working on the Carrie Franklin case."

"What are you talking about?"

"I'm trying to find out where this young woman came from."

"Why?"

"Because you are in love with her, and I am worried about that."

"Dad, I know about her life from the time she was about four years old. She had a great life with Doug and Jane Waters. They did a great job teaching her moral values, and right from wrong. She knows what it is like to be loved."

"How do you know all this?"

"We talked a lot when the four of us had dinner. The Waters told about the child they took into their home, and how she slowly developed into the young woman she is now. A very fine young woman."

Charles smiled at that comment.

"One thing Carrie said surprised me. I was talking about some of the things we did as a family when I was a child. I talked about going to the park where there were swings, seesaws, and sandboxes. Carrie suddenly became very introspective and whispered that she thought she had experienced these same things. That is not possible, of course, because she did not live in Bellfield when she was young."

Maybe she did, Charles thought. *I need to talk with John.*

CHAPTER 51

There was an air of excitement when Maggie, Emma, Nora, and Jane met for their monthly luncheon. There was a lot to talk about. Maggie had invited Maude to attend the luncheon with her. She thought Maude might have some interesting tidbits to add to their discussions. Nancy did not attend because she needed to be at the boutique now that they were shorthanded. Maggie knew that the main topic of conversation at the luncheon would be Jackie. She did not know Nora would be bringing up a different topic.

After the waitress took their orders, Nora spoke up. "I had an interesting person come to my office last week," she stated. "Paul Tennyson, the sergeant from the police department, came in and asked to see the birth records from the mid-1970s. Of course, he did not tell me why he wanted these records."

Maude gasped. All eyes turned toward her. "This comment has to be kept in the strictest confidence," she told everyone. All nodded in solemn agreement. "That same policemen visited John at the rectory. I think he was looking for baptismal records from the same period of time." She hoped no one would ask how she came by that information.

"I had a sense that he did not find what he was looking for at my office," Nora offered. "He seemed frustrated when he left."

Maggie had not intended to tell her friends about Paul's visit to her home, but now she felt compelled to do so. "Paul came to visit me the same week. We had a nice chat, mostly about Carrie. To be honest, I was perplexed by his visit. I have no idea why he came to talk to me."

"We have had some strange things happen ever since your tenant came to town," Emma said.

"My tenant is a very nice woman," Maggie commented defensively. "I am sure she has nothing to do with whatever Sgt. Tennyson is investigating."

"Really! She comes to town supposedly looking for a long-lost cousin. After a while her coworker disappears, and the police start searching for heaven knows what. It all seems connected to me. Before Carrie came to town, no one ever came to the library looking for twenty-year-old newspaper articles."

Nora spoke up. "And no one ever looked for old birth records until Carrie did, and now Sgt. Tennyson."

"I don't recall anyone ever looking for twenty-year-old baptismal records either," Maude offered.

Jane, who had listened to this discussion without comment, spoke up. "Apparently, we have a mystery in our little town. Let's put our heads together and see what we can come up with. How many of you think all of this may have some connection with the disappearance of Jackie?" All hands were raised quickly. Jane continued on. "What do we know about Jackie?" After a brief discussion, they realized that none of them had seen or ever heard of Jackie before she started working at the Unique Boutique. "It is like she materialized out of the blue," Nora remarked.

No one noticed how quiet Maude was.

Maybe I was wrong. Maybe I did not have to take the pearls, one woman thought.

*****

Jackie had no idea she was being discussed by the women in town she often had lunch with. She had no idea of anything. She did not even know where she was, didn't wonder if anyone was looking for her. She couldn't think, could hardly move. She had not had food for days. She dimly recalled that someone would come into the room where she was, give her something to drink through a straw, then give her a shot. She no longer protested the shot. She knew it would do no good. The next time, she was going to refuse to drink from the straw. She had no reason to go on living.

CHAPTER 52

JANE FILLED ED IN ON all the comments made at the ladies' luncheon. "Do you think something strange is going on in this town?" she asked her husband.

"I have no idea. I do wonder about the real reason why Carrie Franklin moved to this town. I don't think anyone believes the cousin story. And I am worried about Jackie Patnode. It seems surprising to me that she has been gone for about four days, and no one knows her whereabouts or has heard from her. I have no idea why Paul Tennyson would be searching old birth records unless it has something to do with Jackie's disappearance."

"There is something else I am wondering about also. Last week, we printed a real estate transfer for that old house on Brook Street, but I have not seen any activity there. The house will need a lot of work to make it habitable. Why would someone purchase the property, then just let it sit there as is?"

Why indeed? Jane thought.

A similar discussion was being held in the Abbot household. Maude had to be very careful as she told John about the discussions held at the luncheon. She certainly did not want him to suspect that she had looked to see what Paul Tennyson had been researching at the rectory a few days earlier. "As you can imagine," she said, "the main topic of discussion was the disappearance of Jackie Patnode. Nora Ryan told us that Paul Tennyson went to the town clerk's office to research birth records from twenty years ago. Do you think that would have anything to do with Jackie? I assume the police department is searching for her."

"Why a search? She is probably just fine. She is probably on vacation, and just didn't think to tell anyone."

"The Reardons would know if she was on vacation."

"That is true. By the way, don't forget that anything that happens here at the rectory is confidential. I hope you did not tell your friends that Sgt. Tennyson did some research here."

"I know better than to do that."

I didn't lie, Maude thought. *I do know better. I just don't always do what I know I should.*

CHAPTER 53

RICK THOUGHT THE YOUNG GIRL who entered the boutique looked familiar. *No,* he decided, *I don't know her. She must remind me of someone I know. She doesn't look like she can afford anything we have here in the store. I hope I don't have to disappoint her.*

"Can I help you?" Rick asked.

"I am looking for someone named Rick Reardon."

Rick was puzzled by the girl's answer. Why would she be looking for him? "Why are you searching for this person?"

"I think he might be a friend of my, uh, my family." Jen did not want to mention her mother.

"Then your family must know the whereabouts of Rick Reardon."

"No, I don't think they do."

"I'm sorry, young lady. I cannot help you. Is there anything else I can help you with?"

"No, I guess not. Thank you." Jen left the store.

Both Jen and Rick were puzzled by this encounter. Rick's picture with Nancy was in the store window. *Must be she did not see the picture in the window*, Rick thought. *Why is she searching for me, and why does she look familiar?* Jen knew, from seeing the picture when she visited the store earlier, that it was Rick she was speaking to. She could not understand why he did not identify himself. She was a little frightened by this denial.

Jen was hungry, so she had planned to look for a McDonald's, so she could get a burger before her long drive home. As she left the boutique's parking lot, she noticed the Star Restaurant. *I am going to go in there*, she thought. *Maybe I can collect some information about*

Rick Reardon. This is a small town. I bet everyone knows everyone else. Townspeople would certainly know the business owners.

Dawn Raye worked the lunch shift at the Star Restaurant. The job gave her a little extra money, and she was still able to be home when the girls came home from school. She was surprised to see a young girl enter the restaurant alone. Teens usually went to McDonald's, unless they were lunching with their parents.

"Would you like to be seated at a table, or would you prefer sitting at the counter?" Dawn asked Jen.

"The counter is fine." Jen wanted to have an opportunity to talk to Dawn. Jen ordered a burger, fries, and a Coke. She waited impatiently as Dawn waited on customers at a table. When Dawn came back to the counter and began cleaning it, Jen spoke. "That boutique in the mall looks like a really nice store."

"I guess it probably is," Dawn answered. "I have never been in there. I can't afford the prices."

"Is it owned by people who live in town?"

"Yes, it is owned by Nancy and Rick Reardon."

"They must have several employees who work there."

"No." Dawn was a little perplexed by all these questions. "They only have two employees. The owners wait on customers as well as running the place. Actually, there is just one employee now." Dawn corrected her comment.

"I went into the store and was surprised to see a male clerk. It appears that the boutique caters to wealthy women."

"I guess that would be true, but it is not surprising to have the store owner wait on customers."

"But the man I spoke to was not the owner. I asked to speak to Rick Reardon, and the man said he did not know who Rick Reardon was."

Dawn immediately felt uncomfortable about this conversation. "I can't give you any information about the boutique. A few days ago, an employee of the boutique went missing. I have no idea why, or if anyone has been hired to take her place." Dawn handed Jen her check and went to wait on new customers that had just entered the restaurant. Jen left money on the counter and left the restaurant.

He had heard the entire exchange between Jen and Dawn. *Who is this girl?* he wondered. *And why is Rick Reardon lying about his identity? Is this occurrence going to interfere with my plans?*

As Jen drove home, she wondered why an employee of Rick Reardon had disappeared.

CHAPTER 54

A FEW DAYS AFTER CHARLES TALKED with Chuck, he decided to act on his idea of speaking with John Abbott about Carrie Franklin. It was Maude who made the appointment.

When Charles entered John's office, the two men shook hands firmly, demonstrating their mutual respect.

"John," Charles said, "I will be up front with you about my reason for being here. I am here on an investigative mission. My son, Chuck, has fallen in love with Carrie Franklin. I admit I have no idea how she feels about him. I am worried that he will get hurt."

"Chuck is an adult."

"I realize that. He knows I want to learn more about Carrie, and he doesn't seem to mind, even though he has no interest himself in learning more about her. He is truly smitten."

"What do you hope to learn from me?"

"I don't buy Carrie's story that she is searching for a lost cousin that she may or may not have. Neither do I buy the story that she is living here to be close to a community college in New Hampshire. It would serve her better to live in a small New Hampshire community. I think she believes she lived in this town when she was a very small child and that she wants to find out what her life was like here."

"What on earth makes you think that?"

"Why else would she come here? This town has little to offer young people. Then there is a conversation Carrie had recently at dinner with Chuck and her parents that solidified the idea for me. Charles told John about Carrie's whispered statement that she thought she remembered being at the park Chuck described when she was a very young child."

"Do you recall hearing about anything mysterious happening eighteen or so years ago to a child about three years old? Were there any stories about a child disappearing during that time period?"

"I don't recall anything like that. Have you discussed this with your cousin, Nell? She would be the one to know if anything like that happened."

"I could ask, but I don't think she could share any information with me because of confidentiality issues."

"I vaguely remember some story about a child that was found with some injuries. Some believe the child was spirited out of town mysteriously and was never heard of again. I don't believe the story."

"If the story was true, could the child have been Carrie?"

"It is possible. But not probable."

"Thank you for your time, John." Charles got up to leave. He decided he had gotten all the information he could from John. He had a glimmer of hope for finding out more about Carrie now that he knew that a child had disappeared from Bellfield all those years ago. The child would be about the same age that Carrie is now.

Maude had decided that the door that led into John's office needed to be cleaned and that the doorknob needed to be polished at the same time that Charles and John met. This was probably the cleanest door in town. After Charles left, Maude made a phone call.

When he returned to his office, Charles called Nell. It would be another week or so before she and her husband would move to Florida. Charles asked if she knew anything about a little girl who had been injured or who had disappeared from Bellfield. This would be about eighteen years ago, he explained to Nell. Nell responded that she had no recollection of such a case, and could not discuss it if she did.

When they hung up after their conversation, Charles was discouraged, and Nell was alarmed.

That evening, Charles related all that had transpired that day to Chuck and Joan. "Maybe I will attend the next ladies' luncheon," Joan said.

CHAPTER 55

CARRIE KNEW THAT SOMETHING WAS wrong as soon as she entered her apartment. She could smell a light scent similar to a man's cologne. No man has ever been in her apartment except her foster dad, and he seldom used cologne. She walked into the kitchen and immediately noticed that her coffee maker had been moved, and a chair had been pulled out from the table as if someone had been sitting there. She walked into the bedroom, trembling. Her closet door was slightly ajar. She was positive she had closed it tightly in the morning. Nothing else seemed to be amiss.

At that moment, her doorbell rang. The sound made her jump. She was almost afraid to go to the door.

She looked out her door and saw Maggie with Sgt. Tennyson from the Bellfield Police Department. As soon as she opened the door, Maggie started to speak in an agitated voice.

"Carrie," she cried, "why didn't you tell me about the threatening letters you have been receiving?"

"I didn't want to alarm you. I will look for a new apartment and move as soon as possible. I don't want to put you in any danger."

"You will do no such thing. We signed a year's lease, and I want both of us to honor it. Sgt. Tennyson is going to look out for us."

Paul spoke up. "Today Maggie received a letter similar to the ones you have been receiving. I felt it necessary to show her the copies of the ones you have received. I hope you understand."

"I do. But there is a new problem that I discovered just before you came to the door. Please come inside."

Carrie stepped back so that Paul and Maggie could enter the apartment. "Someone has been inside my apartment." She pointed to the coffee maker. "Someone moved my coffee maker after I left for work. They also moved this kitchen chair and opened the door of the closet in the bedroom."

"Are you absolutely sure you did not do these things yourself?" Paul asked.

"Yes, I am. I really need to move. I don't want to put Maggie in danger."

"If you do, you will be playing right into the hands of the person who wants to frighten you. I think you need to see this." Paul took a letter from his pocket. It was written in block print just like the letters Carrie and Jackie had received. It said:

> YOU NEED TO GET CARRIE FRANKLIN OUT OF YOUR GARAGE APARTMENT. YOU HAVE THIRTY DAYS OR WILL SUFFER THE CONSEQUENCES.

Carrie was stunned to learn that Maggie had received this letter. "I must leave at once. I don't want Maggie to be frightened or upset because of me."

"Carrie, right now I need to have someone check this apartment for fingerprints. We are also checking the letters you and Maggie received for prints, then we will go from there." Paul was careful not to mention the letters Jackie had received.

"I hope you will drop your plans to move, at least for the near future. You and Maggie can watch out for each other. Also, it will be easier to check on the two of you if you are in the same place."

"I am working hard to locate the sender of your letters, and will work just as hard to determine who may have been in your apartment today. Please be patient. It will take some time to do this."

Paul purposely did not tell Carrie and Maggie that Jackie had received similar letters before her disappearance. He did not want them to worry about their welfare, even though he was very worried about them. *I will be keeping a very close eye on these two,* he thought.

CHAPTER 56

NELL WARNER AND HER HUSBAND, Frank, were planning to move to Florida as soon as Nell retired.

Frank had been on the Bellfield police department for thirty years. He loved his work but was tired of the cold winters. He was not ready to retire completely, but he knew it was time for him to slow down. He was currently in Florida to complete paperwork for his new job as a part-time deputy in a small county sheriff's office. At the same time, he was searching for a condo for him and Nell to purchase as soon as she was able to join him in Florida. He dreaded the hassle of the move from Vermont to Florida, but once the move was completed it would be possible for him and Nell to relax and enjoy their new life together.

Both he and Nell had been very dedicated to their jobs and both had worked very long hours. Social work and police work both required long hours. *No wonder we never had kids*, he thought, *we did not have a lot of time to be together even though we were deeply in love.*

While Frank was away, Nell decided to call her cousin, Charles Warner, and plan a get-together before she moved out of state. Their busy lives had prevented them from seeing a lot of each other in the past years, though they were devoted to each other.

When Nell called, she invited Joan, Charles, and Chuck out to dinner. "I can't entertain in my home because everything is packed for the move to Florida," she explained.

"Why don't we have dinner here?" Joan suggested. "We can relax and talk over coffee and not worry about lingering too long at a restaurant while other people are waiting patiently for a table." They planned to get together the next Friday evening.

Nell was greeted warmly when she arrived at Joan and Charles' home the next Friday evening.

"Chuck wants me to express his regrets for not being here this evening," Charles told Nell. He is away at a golf weekend with friends. The weekend has been planned for several weeks."

"No problem," Nell responded. "He should be out with friends his own age. How is he doing? I understand he is a tremendous asset to your law firm. You must be very proud of him."

"I am," Charles told Nell. "He is an excellent jurist and will continue to improve as he gains experience."

"Does he still live here?"

"He has his own apartment in what used to be the guest suite of the house. He is very independent and insists on paying rent for his apartment."

"Is there a woman in his life, or am I being rude by asking?"

"He dates often," Joan answered, "but there has never been anyone special. I wish there was. I would love to have grandchildren."

"Be patient," Charles chided. "He is only twenty-five. I do think he is getting interested in a young woman who recently moved to town."

"Tell me about her."

"Her name is Carrie Franklin. Her story is that she has moved to Bellfield for two reasons. One is to locate someone who she believes may be a long-lost cousin. She has done extensive research at the library and town clerk's office, looking for that person. She has also been seen walking through the cemetery, reading the names on the gravestones. The other reason she says she moved here is because Bellfield is close to a community college over the border in New Hampshire she hopes to attend someday."

"You sound like you do not entirely believe her story."

"I believe she is here searching for something, but not a long-lost cousin. In addition, she would be better off living in a community in New Hampshire if she wants to attend college there. She would not have to pay out-of-state tuition."

"Maybe she is not someone you would want Chuck to be involved with," Nell suggested.

Joan chimed in, "Oh, there is nothing sinister about her. She is a very sweet girl."

"What did you say her name is?"

"Carrie Franklin."

The name Carrie triggered something in Nell's mind, but she immediately lost it.

"Let's go in for dinner now," Joan suggested. "I want to hear all about your retirement. What do you reflect on when you think back on your career? You have the reputation of being an outstanding social worker. Many children have better lives because of your work. You must feel very proud of that."

"I feel confident about what I have accomplished over the past years. Of course, my work is very confidential, so I cannot say a lot. I do believe I have helped a lot of children by being able to remove them from abusive situations and placing them in warm, loving homes. I will always be bothered by the cases that did not turn out well for some children. Those cases will stay with me for the rest of my life"

"Nell, you need to let these cases go, and enjoy your retirement with Frank."

"I will thoroughly enjoy my retirement with my husband, but will never be able to forget those cases. I can't say a lot, but I am especially concerned about a case of sexual abuse of a very young child. This case was never solved. An event recently happened that might have some bearing on that case. Someone called trying to get information on a child. Naturally, I did not respond to the caller. I am convinced the call was about that case that is nearly twenty years old. There would be no reason for anyone to call about any of my other cases. The call both encouraged and frightened me. Encouraged because I would like to see the case reopened, and frightened because I do not want anyone to do anything to hurt this child who would be a young adult now. Anyway, let's talk about something else."

"You are right, Nell. Tell me about your new home."

Neither woman noticed how thoughtful Charles had become.

CHAPTER 57

At their next weekly meeting, Carrie told Scott about the dinner conversation between Chuck, her parents, and herself. She told him about the feeling she had that she had been to the park on the west side of the town that Chuck described.

"Carrie," Scott said, "do you honestly believe that you might have lived in this town as a very young child?"

"I don't know. If I never lived here, why would I have that feeling that I had played in the park Chuck described? And why do I have that strong aversion to the old house on Brook Street?' Do you think maybe I have been in that house? Did something bad happen to me there?"

And why did someone you work with disappear just a few months after you moved into the town? Scott thought.

"Carrie, how would you feel about visiting West Side Park?

"I am not sure I would know how to find it."

"I do. I will drive you there. Let me call Nan and tell her I will be about a half hour late for dinner, and we will be on our way."

"Did Nan mind that you will be late for dinner? Carrie asked after Scott hung up the phone.

"Nan never minds thing like this. She is a very sweet and understanding wife."

I wonder if anyone will ever think of me like that, Carrie thought.

Carrie jumped out of Scott's car as soon as they arrived at West Side Park. She ran first to a sandbox that was situated behind a set of swings. "I used to play here," she said. "I had a red pail and shovel. My mother would laugh at my antics. When I tired of playing in the sandbox, she would push me high up on the swings."

Carrie was quiet for a moment, then she began to shriek. "Where is my mother, Scott? Where is my mother?"

CHAPTER 58

Paul Tennyson was disappointed, but not surprised, to learn that no fingerprints were found on any of the letters received by Carrie, Jackie, or Maggie. It appeared, but could not be proven, that all the letters were typed on the same device. Paul and others in his department were investigating the backgrounds of people in his town that had something suspicious in their backgrounds eighteen or twenty years ago that might make them nervous about Jackie and/or Carrie being residents of their town. Two of the names his detectives came up with shocked him. The names were Charles Warner and John Abbott. The third name, Rick Reardon, did not surprise him.

Paul made an appointment to see Charles Warner.

Charles had no idea why a sergeant from the police department wanted to meet with him. He assumed it had to have something to do with one of his clients, but he was puzzled by that. None of his current clients had criminal backgrounds.

Charlie's office had a nook under a bay window where he had placed two wing chairs with a coffee table between the chairs. He used this setting when he expected his meeting to be casual. Paul and Charles shook hands, and Charles indicated that Paul should sit in one of the wing chairs. He offered coffee, but Paul declined.

"What can I do for you, Sgt. Tennyson?"

"I am investigating a criminal case, the details of which I cannot share with you. I need to ask you some questions."

"If the questions concern one of my clients, I will have to be very careful of my answers because of client/lawyer confidentiality issues."

"My questions have nothing to do with your law practice."

"Then I am puzzled as to why you are here."

"I need to ask questions about your background."

"Why?"

"I can't divulge the reasons at this particular time."

Charles decided to cooperate and answer Paul's questions. He could stop the discussion any time that he began to feel uncomfortable. "If you have been doing your job, Sgt. Tennyson, you know all about my background. I was born here in Bellfield, attended schools here. In high school, I was the captain of the football team, graduated fifth in my class, and was named to the National Honor Society. I attended UVM in Burlington, then attended Harvard Law School. After I earned my degree and passed the bar exam, I moved back here to open my law practice. The rest is history."

"What about your wife?"

Charles was becoming more and more agitated by Paul's questions.

"What do you mean, what about my wife?"

"What is her background?"

"Again, I am sure you already know the answers to these questions. She grew up here in Bellfield, she graduated high school third in the class. She still teases me about graduating ahead of me. After high school, she attended UVM, moving back here after graduation. I guess we would be considered small-town people."

"When did you start dating your wife?"

"I am sure you know we were high school sweethearts. Things cooled off a bit during our college years, but we did keep in touch. We started dating again as soon as we both returned to Bellfield after college. We were married a year later."

"Do you have a history of sexual discretions while attending UVM?"

Charles stood up after this question was posed. "This interview is over," he said. "My secretary will show you out."

That was a much stronger reaction to my question than I expected, Paul thought as he left Charles's office.

CHAPTER 59

Paul knew that his next interview had to be with John Abbott. His detective team had discovered some troubling information about events that had occurred at the rectory about twenty years before. Paul hoped to learn more about these events from John.

Of course, it was Maude who ushered Paul into John's office, and of course she was curious about the conversation that would happen between the two men. John made sure the door was firmly shut as soon as Maude exited the room.

"I am going to be blunt about why I am here," Paul told John. "I am investigating some troubling events that are currently happening in this town. My detectives have been investigating events that took place in Bellfield about twenty years ago. They have uncovered some information that led them to believe these two things may have a connection. The events from twenty years ago are not conducive to church teachings. What can you tell me about these events?"

John blanched, but he was able to keep his voice steady. "I have no idea what you are talking about."

"I believe you do. There was some scandal about a young girl who was a member of your church. There seems to have been a cover-up about this event. Nothing was done to help this girl get through whatever trauma she suffered. The family eventually disappeared."

John recalled that twenty years ago he was on the phone trying to right a terrible wrong when his brother Michael walked into the room. He asked Michael how much of the conversation he had heard.

"Enough to own you for life," Michael had answered. John was not going to let something like that happen to him again. "Twenty years is a long time, Paul. You cannot expect me to recall all the incidents of that time, but if a family from my parish had disappeared, I would certainly remember that."

Paul was not going to let John off that easily. He knew John was lying; he just did not know why. "Do you know that a page from your baptismal Bible is missing?"

"That cannot be true."

"It is. My detectives noticed that a page was missing when they were doing their investigations."

"No page from that Bible is missing. We can resolve that problem right now." John retrieved the Bible that had been in use during the last fifteen to twenty years. He was shocked to find that the page for June 6, 1997, had been torn out of the book. His hand shook as he turned the book for Paul to see that a page was indeed missing. "I have no idea how that page went missing," he stated.

"Do you recall any of the names on that page?"

"I do not," John lied.

Then he said to himself, *How could two such sweet little girls go so wrong?*

*****

Jackie heard a noise. She didn't even know where the noise came from. She knew she had food to eat and water to drink, but she did not know how it got on the floor beside her.

She felt a prick. "Here is you medicine, Jackie." The voice said. "It won't be long now. Sgt. Tennyson is getting too nosy. Both you and the little girl will be out of the picture soon."

CHAPTER 60

Pat Lawrence had not thought about her sister for a very long time: months, if not years. *I can't imagine why I am thinking of her now,* Pat said to herself. *We never did get along very well, and when we became older, I guess our lives went in such different directions that we lost touch.*

She never told Jenny that she had an aunt. Jenny believed that all the family she had was her mother and her maternal grandparents from whom Pat had been estranged for many years. *My parents could not tolerate my attitude about my sister, and that was caused the rift between us*, Pat always told herself. *The fact that I became pregnant out of wedlock was the straw that broke the camel's back. My parents have pretty much ignored me ever since that happened,* Pat thought. *It is strange that Jenny never asked about her father's family. It is a good thing I did not have to fabricate more lies. Jenny must never learn the truth about her birth. I must stop her visits to Bellfield. The trouble began when she found the article about Rick. How stupid of me to keep it.*

Out of wedlock for sure, Pat mused. He was married and had no intention of losing his wealthy wife. *And there was no love between us, just respect on my part. He mentored me and was always professional except for that one slip up. And that is what it was. There was no emotional bond between us. He was a father figure to me. A role my own father could never fulfill. He was too busy climbing the corporate ladder. It was when Rick told me that my father really did love me but was too busy to show it that the incident happened. I was sobbing uncontrollably, and he put his arms around me to console me. One thing led to another, and the result was Jenny. It was not an assault. I was a willing partner.*

As Pat was thinking about her past, her phone rang. "This is Pat Lawrence." She always answered the phone in this manner. It made things easier if it was a business call. Pat worked as an agent for a real estate company. She loved her job, and would be eternally grateful to her employers of nearly two decades for allowing her to work many hours out of her home when Jenny was little.

"This is Rick."

"What do you want?"

"I called to warn you that the past is being dug up here in Bellfield. You may want to prepare your daughter for some upsetting revelations. I will try to diffuse any questions about what happened between us, but I may not be successful. Our little mistake ruined my life, I don't want it to ruin anyone else's." Rick hung up.

Pat sat down shaking. She was still sitting by the phone when Jenny burst into the room.

"Mom," she said excitedly, "I secretly took pictures of the people who work at the Unique Boutique, the shop in Bellfield I told you about." She handed the phone with the pictures on it to her mother. "Do you know any of these people?"

Pat nearly fainted.

CHAPTER 61

THE LADIES OF BELLFIELD MET at the Star Restaurant for their monthly luncheon. They were pleased to welcome Joan Warner to their group. "Charles and Chuck are out of town meeting with a potential client," she explained. "I thought it would be nice to meet for lunch and not have to eat alone."

Everyone gave their luncheon order to the waitress, then proceeded to discuss family issues and town affairs. Then the subject of Jackie Patnode came up.

"Has anyone heard from Jackie Patnode?" Nora Ryan asked. "I don't think that she has been working at the boutique for quite a while now."

"She has not been there for a week or two," Emma Perkins offered. "Not that I ever go in there to shop. No one with a librarian's pay can afford their merchandise. But I do like to go there occasionally to window-shop just for the fun of it. A girl can dream, right? Jackie always smiles and waves when she sees me. She hasn't appeared to be in the shop the last few times I have walked by."

"I think something strange is going on," Maude said. "I don't know why, but Sgt. Tennyson has been asking a lot of questions about both Jackie and the new girl, Carrie Franklin."

Carrie will be the "new girl" until someone more interesting shows up in town, Maggie thought as she listened to what Maude had to say. She went on to say, "I wonder if there is some connection between Jackie and Carrie. Maybe it has something to do with the fact that they both work for the Reardons. Rick Reardon has a questionable past. We all know that no self-respecting father in this community would allow his daughter to work at the boutique. No one really knows where either Jackie or Carrie come from. How did they both end up at the boutique?"

Joan Warner was relieved to learn that Paul Tennyson was talking to people other than Charles.

She thought he was being questioned because of Charles's history at UVM. However, she made no comment.

Maggie was getting upset about Maude's comments about Jackie and Carrie. *What is wrong with me?* she thought. *Why am I feeling so ill?*

The ladies at the luncheon were not the only ones discussing Jackie Patnode.

CHAPTER 62

Carrie carefully lifted the dresses from the most recent shipment to the boutique. She hung the dresses, blouses, and skirts on hangers in the front of the store, so they could be seen from the windows. She then placed the accessories on shelves near the new merchandise so that customers viewing the dresses, skirts, and blouses could not possibly miss seeing the accessories that would complement them. She did not realize that Rick and Nancy were watching her every move, and were pleased with what they saw.

"Carrie can easily replace Jackie if she does not return to work," Nancy told Rick.

"She can, but the workload is too much for one person. We would have to hire another person."

"And just how do you think we would be able to do that?" Nancy asked sarcastically.

Rick did not answer that question. Instead, he picked up the phone and called Paul Tennyson.

"What information have you learned about Jackie Patnode?" Rick asked when Paul answered his call.

"Very little," Paul answered. "Of course, after I went to Jackie's apartment in response to your request for a wellness check, the chief and I agreed to begin to investigate her disappearance as a missing-persons case. I and some of my staff have completed a background check and researched bank information, social security history, driver's license information, and medical history. I have interviewed several members of this town who have lived here more than twenty years. I have learned nothing about Jackie. It is as if she materialized on this earth the day she arrived at your shop."

"There must be some information about Jackie out there somewhere," Rick said hopefully.

"Well, there isn't, and I believe you know why. I don't believe you are being candid with me. I don't believe your story that Jackie showed up at your shop seeking employment and that you hired her on the spot. Why didn't you hire a local girl?"

Rick believed that Paul knew the answer to that question.

"If there is anything I can do to help, please call me," Rick said as he hung up the phone.

"You could tell the truth," Paul said to the air. *I just hope the woman is not in danger,* he thought.

*****

Jackie stirred. *Why is he doing this?* she asked herself. He had not been in for several hours to give her a drink and a shot, so Jackie was able to think more clearly. *I have seen him at church and at church socials. I believed he was a pillar of the community, so I trusted him. When he came to my apartment and told me he had information about my past, I felt comfortable letting him in. I don't remember much after that. Where is my child? I must be crazy. I don't have a child.*

CHAPTER 63

"Carrie," Scott said at their next meeting, "I think we both have the sense that you must have lived in Bellfield at some time. Your foster parents believe you may have come from here, though they are not sure why they believe that. Also, you seem to have some connection with that old house on Brook Street. You would not have the strong reaction to the house if that were not true. The most telling argument that you may have lived here at some time is what you said when Chuck was talking about the park in the west side of town. That comment that you remember being there was very telling."

"I have tried and tried to remember my past before I went into foster care, but I cannot recall anything."

"I believe that whatever happened to you before foster care happened when you were very young. Too young to recall that time in your life. It is a beautiful afternoon. Let's take a walk." Scott phoned Nan to tell her that he would be out of the office for a while. When he hung up the phone, he was smiling. "My wife is bored," he said. "Before I go home for dinner, I will have to stop at the store and buy her a book to read. She is getting so big that she has to rest often. She doesn't watch much TV, so she has to have something to occupy her mind." Scott smiled broadly as he spoke about his wife.

Scott and Carrie walked to the house on Brook Street. Scott could see Carrie begin to shake as they neared the house. He gently encouraged her to walk up the sidewalk to the steps. Carrie resisted, but Scott took her arm gently and urged her forward. As she reached the top step, she began to cry uncontrollably. "No hurt, baby," She sobbed.

He was watching this scene carefully. *I may have to step up my plans,* he thought.

CHAPTER 64

When Paul returned to his office, he contacted Chief Jacobs.

"What's up, Paul?"

"I think we need to put more time into investigating our missing-persons case."

"For what reason?"

Paul again filled the chief in on everything he had learned about Jackie. He told the chief about his interviews with John Abbott, Charles Warner, and Rick Reardon. He also discussed his search for information about Carrie.

"As strange as it seems," Paul told the chief, "it appears that neither Carrie Franklin nor Jackie Patnode existed before they arrived in Bellfield."

"So what are you planning to do from here?"

"I guess I need to interview everyone again. I did not mention the letters to anyone before. I think I need to do it this time, and need to let them know that we now have a missing-persons case, and a possible crime scene. That will probably make them nervous."

"Who are you the most suspicious of?"

"I don't know. John Abbott seems to have a pristine background, but he was definitely nervous during our interview. I think he was hiding something. I think his wife was trying to listen into our conversation."

"There is something about Rick Reardon's background that is very suspicious. Why did he leave the church so suddenly?"

"Charles Warner had an incident when he was in college that makes him suspect. He became very irritated when I asked him about his wife's college days."

"Keep me informed of your investigation." The chief indicated that the meeting was over.

Paul decided to speak with Nell first. "Nell, can we meet for coffee somewhere? Somewhere where we can speak in private?"

"You can come here. My husband is out golfing. He wants to improve his game before we move to Florida where he will compete with snowbirds who have been playing all year long."

Paul realized how hungry he was when he walked into Nell's kitchen and smelled freshly baked blueberry muffins and freshly brewed coffee.

"Paul, I was surprised that you called again. I explained to you the last time we talked that I cannot give you any information about the cases I worked on as a social worker. Unless, of course, you have a warrant signed by a judge giving you permission to review certain files. The files are all at the DCYS office at the town hall. In that case, you will have to deal with my replacement."

"I would be very surprised if you had any information on the people I want to speak with you about. How much do you know about the Unique Boutique?"

"No more than anyone else in town. Most of us can't afford to shop there. Only the people who live on the west side of town, in those large mansions, can afford their prices."

"In that case, how do you think the shop survives in a town like Bellfield?"

"I don't know. Maybe there is money somewhere in the owner's background. Old money."

"That is possible but not probable. What do you know specifically about the employees there?"

"Very little. I believe the older one, Jackie Patnode, moved here to work at the boutique.

"Where did she come from?"

"I have no idea."

"That is the point. I have investigated her thoroughly, and it appears that she did not exist before coming here to town."

"That is impossible."

"But no one, even Jackie herself, knows where she came from. She doesn't recall anything before coming to in the rehab center. She received a letter offering her a job at the boutique here in town. In the letter was enough cash to get her to Bellfield and support her until she began earning a salary."

"How did you learn that?"

"From Jackie herself. She asked me not to reveal that information to anyone. I have kept that promise until right now. I know you will be discreet."

Nell nodded.

"Now let's discuss the other employee at the boutique, Carrie Franklin. Her background is also nebulous. She has no idea where she lived before going into foster care at about the age of four. For some reason a person, or persons unknown, did everything they could to obscure her background. Do you think that person, or those persons, could be you and me?"

Nell blanched. "I need to speak with someone," she said.

When Paul left, he realized he had not told Nell about the threatening letters that both Carrie and Jackie had received.

CHAPTER 65

After Paul left her home, Nell made a phone call that she knew would be very difficult. The call needed to be completed before her husband came home. She never kept any secrets from him, but this call was work related, and he understood that she could not discuss that part of her life with him.

Nell got right to the point when her call was answered. "Twenty years ago, we helped each other out of two very difficult situations. I am not sure if what we did was right, but it seemed it was all we could do at the time. We had to help some very vulnerable people. But now I think we have to right some wrongs."

"I don't think so. One girl was saved and is living a pretty normal life. We do not want to disrupt that. I admit the other might be in very grave danger, but there is nothing we can do to change that. Why this call after all these years? We admitted that someday someone might recall some of what happened to them. All we can do is sit back and watch the results."

"Jackie disappeared for several years. We have no idea where she was or what she was doing all that time. That concerns me, John."

"If you recall, Jackie ran from the hospital a couple of days after she was taken there. When she was brought to the hospital, she had no idea what her name was, could tell us nothing about herself. We think she ran because she was so doped up that she was confused about who she was and where she was. She might have been afraid of something."

"How did you find her?"

"I volunteered, doing counseling in rehab centers within a fifty-mile radius of here, hoping to find her. I finally got lucky."

"When you found her, what did she tell you about herself?"

"Absolutely nothing! She has total amnesia. She does not recall anything before waking up in the rehab center. The doctors believe she may be blocking out something in her past."

"We know that is true."

"I am not sure. I don't think she knew anything that was happening around her at that time. Either she drugged herself into a stupor, or someone did it to her, so she wouldn't be aware of her surroundings."

"What are we going to do about all of this now?"

"Absolutely nothing."

"Maybe you are doing nothing, but I feel I must take some action. However, at this point I don't know what that action will be."

"Let's think this through for a few days. We don't want to do something rash that we will regret for many years."

Nell hung up, feeling very dissatisfied with the conversation.

Maude made another phone call.

CHAPTER 66

SHE ENTERED THE UNIQUE BOUTIQUE for just the second time in her life. She walked around the shop for a few minutes without being noticed. Carrie was busy changing a display, making room for new merchandise. Rick and Nancy were in the office, deciding which merchandise they should order for the upcoming Christmas season.

She wistfully fingered some of scarves and gloves, wondering what it would be like to be able to afford such lovely accessories. She was startled when Carrie came up to her.

"Can I help you?" she asked.

"Oh no, my dear. I was just looking over some of these beautiful items you have on display. I could see you were busy and did not want to bother you."

"I came in to tell you that next month's luncheon will mark the twentieth year that our little group has been getting together at the Star Restaurant. The owners are planning a special treat for us to mark the occasion. They really appreciate our patronage. We all hope that you and Nancy can have lunch with us on that special day."

"Thank you," Carrie answered. "That is very kind of you. I am not sure we will be able to attend. It will depend on how busy we are at that time since we are shorthanded right now. I will certainly tell Nancy about your kind invitation."

"Have you heard from Jackie?"

"We have not yet, but hope to soon," Carrie answered evasively.

"Well, I hope you can attend the luncheon. Give my best to Nancy."

She couldn't wait to get out of the shop!

CHAPTER 67

Carrie frowned as she listened to Scott's proposal. He wanted to invite Chuck and Carrie to have dinner with him and Nan at their home.

"I have not had much experience with a dinner for four."

"I know. I know you have no social life. You need to begin to do things that other young women your age do. As far as I can see, all you do is work, have an occasional lunch with Nan, and sometimes have lunch with women three times your age. You can't improve your social skills without practice. There is no better way for you to start than to start with people you are comfortable with. Are you uncomfortable with the fact that I have invited Chuck Warner to complete our little foursome? How do you feel about him? I know he thinks the world of you. You can see it in his eyes when the two of you are in the same room. I think he may be falling in love with you, if he hasn't already. How do you feel about him?"

"I don't know. I worry that I may never be able to develop a normal relationship with a man. I enjoy being with Chuck. He is funny and makes me laugh. He is not like Pete. Pete was demanding and impatient. He wanted our relationship to proceed faster than I was ready for. Chuck does not demand anything from me. He is patient and kind.

Scott liked everything he heard Carrie say. It appeared that Chuck understood Carrie and her problems thoroughly, and was able and willing to work with her. Only a man truly in love could be that understanding.

"Carrie, I think we need to be open and honest with Chuck about why you arrived here in town. I also think he needs to be told about the threatening letters you have been receiving. It is only fair that he knows everything about the girl he is falling love with. The three of us can talk privately sometime if you are not comfortable sharing the information about the letters with Nan."

"Absolutely not. Nan was the first person I felt comfortable talking to after I moved here to Bellfield. She should know everything that the rest of us know." Scott was relieved and happy that Carrie felt that way.

A week later, Chuck picked up Carrie at her apartment, and they drove to Scott and Nan's home for dinner.

Nan served cocktails with crackers and cheese while dinner finished cooking. "No cocktail for me," Nan stated. "It would not be good for little Scott Junior."

"None for me either," Carrie said. "I am not used to drinking alcohol. Nan, I will help you with dinner."

"No serious talk during dinner," Scott stated as they sat down to the table. "We need to enjoy this beautiful roast-beef dinner Nan has prepared. We can talk later over pie and coffee."

Dinner conversation was light and enjoyable. The men laughed as they discussed playing Little League in their younger years. The most serious issue discussed was whether the Red Sox would make the playoffs. Opinions were mixed.

After they finished eating, the men retired to the living room, and Carrie helped Nan clear the table.

"Let me load the dishwasher," Carrie told Nan laughingly. "I can bend down easier that you can."

I wonder if I will ever get to the time that I will want to have a child, Carrie wondered wistfully. A picture of Chuck swam before her eyes.

Once the food was put away in the refrigerator and the dishwasher was loaded, Nan and Carrie joined the men in the living room, bringing pie and coffee.

"My wife makes the best chocolate cream pie in in the whole world," Scott bragged. Carrie could not help noticing the look of affection that passed between Scott and Nan.

"Chuck," Scott said, "Carrie and I have agreed to share with you some information about her life, about which you may not be aware."

"Do you want me to leave the room?" Nan asked.

"Absolutely not," Scott and Carrie chimed in simultaneously.

"Do you want me to talk, Carrie, or do you want to start?"

"You go ahead."

"Chuck, Carrie did not come here to Bellfield to locate a cousin she recently heard about."

Chuck smiled, remembering his recent conversation with his dad.

"She came here," Scott continued, "because her foster parents believe she may have lived here as a very small child. Probably before she was placed in foster care. They have no proof of this, but they recall seeing a phone number with Bellfield's exchange among some of Carrie's belongings.

"As soon as she arrived in town, Carrie searched town records and newspaper accounts of the time she may have lived here, but she found no clues to her identity."

Chuck spoke up. "Carrie, I hope this won't upset you, but my father did the same thing with no success."

"I don't mind, I guess, but why on earth would he do that?"

"He was worried about me. No matter how old you get, you will always be someone's child. He understands how I feel about you."

The room was quiet for a minute or two, then Carrie continued with her story.

"Some things have happened since I arrived here in Bellfield that make me believe I do have some connection with the town. I have an eerie, inexplicable fear of the old abandoned house on Brook Street.

"How does that happen?" Chuck asked.

"When I walk by the house, I become nervous and shaky. Almost faint. If I attempt to walk up the walk, I panic. Scott walked me up to the steps last weeks, and I said something strange. I said, 'Don't hurt baby.' Why would I say something like that?"

"I recall," Chuck interrupted, "that when we had dinner with your parents, I talked about playing, as a child, at the park on the west side of town you said that you thought you had been there. I didn't know what to make of that comment."

"Something more serious has been happening," Scott told Chuck and Nan. "Carrie has been receiving threatening letters advising her to get out of town."

Chuck was obviously very agitated by this news. "Scott, what has been done about this situation? They need to be shown to the police." He turned to Carrie, "Honey, you could be in danger."

Everyone noticed the term of endearment, but no one made any comment.

"The police department has the letters," Carrie assured Chuck. Paul Tennyson is trying to learn where they originated from, but so far, hasn't been successful."

Carried wanted to move away from this conversation. "Nan, she said this has been a wonderful evening. Everything was delicious, and the company warm and friendly, but l think it is time for Chuck and me to leave. You must be tired." She helped Nan take the dessert dishes to the kitchen, and she and Chuck started home.

Chuck was quiet as he drove Carrie to her apartment. He wondered if there was any connection between Carrie's letters and Paul Tennyson's visit to his dad. *There can't be a connection*, he decided.

When they arrived at Carrie's apartment, Chuck insisted on seeing her inside and having Carrie check through the apartment to be sure everything was okay before he left. He wanted to kiss her goodnight, but he knew better than to try.

CHAPTER 68

John Abbott sat at his desk with his head in his hands, wondering what to do next. He thought back to the events of twenty years ago when he had two unsurmountable problems. A young girl pregnant, a young child assaulted. It would have been easier if the two problems had not become intertwined. It would have been easier if he had seen Michael in the doorway. How stupid of him not to shut the door tightly. Maude was out shopping, and as far as he knew, no one else was in the rectory. *How did Michael manage to slip in unnoticed?* John asked himself.

To complicate things, Michael had heard John's side of two conversations, completely misinterpreting both. John's hands were tied. The conversations were privileged, and John could not tell Michael the truth. *I have paid for this event ever since*, John thought.

Was Rick Reardon involved in both events? One was a sixteen-year-old girl, the other a child just past toddler stage. The first was a moment of weakness that has cost Rick dearly ever since. He would have lost his livelihood if he had not been married to a very wealthy woman who owned a thriving business. How can I get this question answered? *John wondered.*

John decided to invite Rick to lunch. "Let's meet at the Star on Wednesday."

"No, it would be better if we meet somewhere out of town, Rick answered. We are not the best of friends. If people in town saw us together at the Star, they would wonder why we were meeting."

John agreed, and they met a few days later at a diner in a little town on the New Hampshire, Vermont, town line named Mapleton. The diner, called Buds, had a reputation for serving delicious sandwiches. Both John and Rick agreed that the reputation was well-deserved.

"Do we have a particular reason for meeting for this little luncheon?" Rick asked.

John got right to the point. "We need to revisit the actions we took when you made your little mistake twenty years ago."

"Why?"

"Because Paul Tennyson is looking into events that occurred during that time period. He is going to thoroughly investigate any events that seem unusual to him."

"I have already warned the woman that she must be prepared in case she is asked questions about that time in her life."

John was shocked by this revelation. "I thought you agreed not to have any contact with that person when we, at the time, had the problem solved?"

"I did not have any contact with her until a couple of months ago when she contacted me. After that, I had her phone number on my caller ID."

"Why on earth did she get in touch with you after all these years? Was she looking for money?"

"No, somehow her daughter found out about me and the boutique, and she has been nosing around. She has come into the boutique, I think, two times. Pat was alarmed and called to let me know what was happening. Unfortunately, Nancy also knows about that call."

John decided to change the subject. He was not sure if this new information would have any effect on what he was trying to accomplish. "Have you been interviewed by Paul Tennyson lately?"

"Yes, but he has no way of knowing about Pat and the kid. In case you're interested, the girl's name is Jenny."

John was obviously upset by this news.

"What is wrong?"

"Jenny was Pat's maternal grandmother's first name. Pat never knew her. I wonder how she came up with that name?"

"Probably just a coincidence."

I don't believe in coincidences."

"We've gotten off the track here," Rick noted. "Why are we really having this lunch and conversation? I don't believe it is to discuss Jenny's great-grandmother's first name."

Neither did I before this, John thought.

"We are here to discuss the events of twenty years ago. I am sure Paul Tennyson will soon find out about you and Pat. It will not look good for either of us if we don't tell him about it first. We need to come clean about what we did when you impregnated Pat all those years ago."

"That's all water over the dam. The church paid the family handsomely to help with the expense of raising a child, and for the promise to keep everything secret. No one knows about this except the church leaders, Nancy, and the two of us."

And Michael, John thought.

"What are you proposing we do?" Rick asked.

"I think we need to tell Paul Tennyson about your little indiscretion and what transpired twenty years ago." *Maybe it will throw him off the case I am really concerned about,* John told himself.

"What will that accomplish?"

"He may come to believe that Carrie is your daughter, and then may stop his investigation into her background."

"There is still the problem of Jackie Patnode."

"You are right about that."

"Anyway, I have no intention of telling anyone about what happened twenty years ago. Nancy is beginning to forgive and forget. It has taken nearly twenty years. I think she is beginning to fall in love with me again. I have stopped my juvenile, flirty behaviors. I want my wife back. I am not going to let anything spoil that. In addition, I do not want to do anything that will traumatize Pat and Jenny. Jenny knows nothing about her paternal parentage. It needs to stay that way."

Rick put money on the table and left the restaurant without finishing his lunch.

Rick is not going to be any help, John told himself. *I have to stop Paul Tennyson's investigation, but how? I think I may know who hurt the little girl I helped Nell with, but how do I get proof?*

CHAPTER 69

He remembered, twenty years ago, being interested in both girls. The younger one became less appealing after her little tryst with Rick Reardon.

The older girl decided to stay in Bellfield to be near her boyfriend when he came home from Marine boot camp in Cherry Point. The child was the result of a weekend reunion. He never knew about the child. He was killed in a training accident soon after returning to camp.

She was having a difficult time raising the child alone. She did not receive governmental support because she and the child's father were never married.

She was fortunate to be hired by an older lady in the community who required assistance, so she could stay in her home. She did light housekeeping chores and prepared meals for her employer to be placed in the freezer to be heated up and eaten later. The kindly woman allowed her to keep the child with her while working. The employer delighted in playing with the child while the mother completed her chores. It was an ideal situation for all parties.

When the woman passed away a couple of years later, she left the mother and child a small amount of money. It would been enough to help support the mother and child until the child entered school, and the mother could find other employment.

I was not going to let that happen. I had been patient, now it was my turn to own the girl. I had never intended to use drugs, but the girl spurned all my efforts to become either a lover or a father figure. Once I started the drugs, she never knew what hit her. I owned her and the child, but now things are getting heated up. As I told her, both she and the child must go. I know where the child is.

CHAPTER 70

NELL WAS ALWAYS IMPRESSED WITH the assisted living facility that was now her father's home. Her one regret about moving to Florida was that she would be living so far away from him. She suggested that he move to a similar facility near to her home in Florida, but he adamantly refused.

"I am happy here," he said, "or at least as happy as I can be without your mother. I have friends here, friends that I delight in beating in chess on a regular basis. I am staying right here."

There were two types of patients at the facility: those who had sound bodies but whose minds failed them, and those whose minds were sound but had failed bodies like her father. *I wonder which would be worse,* Nell thought.

Nell's father, Robert Sullivan, was surprised to see his daughter when she walked into the room.

"Where is Frank?" he asked. "I did not realize this was the day we were going out to lunch."

Nell and her husband, Frank, took her father out for lunch several times a month to have seafood. It was something he loved, but did not have often at the assisted living facility. Nell knew her father would really miss these outings when she moved to Florida. They were planning to have seafood lunches delivered to him several times a month after they moved. They had not told him this. It would be a nice surprise for him.

"Our lunch date is for Friday. Frank will be here with me then. I need to discuss something with you in private."

"Sounds serious."

"It has to do with events that occurred twenty years ago when you were a church elder."

"Nell, you know I can't discuss church events with you if decisions were made as a part of my position on the church board, just as you cannot discuss events with me that were a part of your job."

"Dad, will you please hear me out? Some disturbing things have been happening in town that I want you to know about."

Bob Sullivan listened carefully as Nell told him about the arrival of Carrie Franklin into town, about Jackie Patnode's disappearance, and about Paul Tennyson's investigations.

"I can understand why there are questions about the woman named Jackie Patnode, but why an investigation about the young woman named Carrie Franklin?"

"I have no idea," Nell said. She did not know about the letters that possibly linked the two women together.

"Dad, as a church elder, you had the power to solve church-related problems. Are you confident that you always made the right decisions?"

"I am confident that I made the best decision possible considering the resources I had and the circumstances that presented themselves at the time."

"Are you confident that you made all the right decisions that you had to make concerning the children you served all those years?"

"For the most part, yes."

"For the most part?"

"There is one situation I may not have handled well."

"One out of thirty years of work is not bad."

"Dad, you took charge of the situation when Rick Reardon got involved with a young girl from our parish. How did you handle that situation?"

"The board of elders met and decided that the best way to handle the situation was to help the family relocate. That saved both the church and the family involved from shame and embarrassment. The family announced that the father had been offered a job out of town that was too good to refuse. They moved almost immediately."

"Was the family compensated financially?"

"Their moving expenses were paid by the church, and they were provided the funds needed to hold them over until their house here in Bellfield was sold, and they purchased a new home in their new location. A trust fund was set up to pay for the expected child's expenses until she reached twenty-one or graduated from college. We hired an accountant to oversee these funds, so we were sure none of the money was used for anything other than care for the child."

"Have you kept in touch with the family?"

"Not really. The girl and the parents were estranged even before this happened. I understand that the parents live in Florida now, and the girl and the child live in a small town in New Hampshire about fifty miles from here."

"I thought there were two girls in the family."

"There were. The older girl was nineteen years old and refused to move with the family. She was very much in love with a young man who lived here in Bellfield. It was a very sad story. The young man was a marine and was killed in a training accident before they married. I heard there was a child, but I am not sure if that rumor was true."

"Do they still live here in town?"

"No, they left town mysteriously many years ago. I don't believe anyone has heard from them since then."

"Was there an investigation into their disappearance?"

"No, there was no reason for one. Any young adult can choose to move out of town whenever they wish.

And if there were no questions, the church would be spared the embarrassment of having her family's story dredged up again, Nell thought.

"Do you know where they lived when they were here in town?"

"I am not sure. Possibly on Brook Street."

Nell did not want her father to see how shaken up she was at this revelation, so she quickly glanced at her watch.

"Okay, Dad, I need to leave. I am late for a meeting with Frank. We will see you Friday for lunch." She gave her father a quick peck on the cheek and left the room.

Robert Sullivan was not fooled.

CHAPTER 71

As soon as Nell returned home from her visit with her father, she called Paul Tennyson. "We need to talk," she told him.

"I will see you this afternoon."

As soon as she had served coffee to herself and Paul, Nell sat down and started to talk.

"My father served as an elder at John Abbott's church when there was the scandal concerning Rick Reardon and a teenage girl from the parish. He was instrumental in helping to solve the problem. He arranged to have the family move to a new community. He made sure the family was compensated for the expense of the move and buying a new home. A fund was set up to provide for the expense of raising a child for twenty years. An accountant oversees the fund to be sure all the money goes to the raising of the child."

"And because of that," Paul interjected, "John Abbott helped us when we found the young child abandoned on Brook Street. Between the three of us, we were able to expunge all records of the child's existence, so we could be sure that her abuser would never locate her."

"Some of the things we did were not that legitimate."

"And all three of us have been guilt ridden about our actions ever since, and we all hope and pray that the child found a happy home. However, we knew at the time that what we did was the only way to ensure her safety. We had no idea who her abuser was."

"We still don't. Let's move on to another subject for a few minutes. How much do you actually know about the incident with Rick Reardon and the girl?"

"I don't know any more than what you just told me. In fact, I didn't know as much as I do right now."

"Did you know there were two daughters in that family?"

"I did not."

"The older refused to move with the rest of the family." Nell went on to relate the story of the older daughter just as her father had told her.

"How do you know that she disappeared? Maybe she just moved away."

"My father said that one day they were just gone. Nothing was said to anyone that they might be moving. No one has heard a word from them since that time. He thinks that they lived on Brook Street when they lived here in town."

Paul paled. "My lord, what did we do?"

"Are you thinking that the woman and child found on Brook Street so many years ago can be that girl and her child?"

"I hope not, but it is possible that they are."

"I think they are back in town, but not together."

"What makes you think that?"

"I think the older daughter is the person we know as Jackie Patnode. I also think it is possible that the child is Carrie Franklin."

"How did you arrive at that conclusion?"

"I haven't actually concluded that. I just look at it as a possibility."

"That would explain why I couldn't locate any information about Carrie Franklin."

"Or about Jackie Patnode. We did our job well."

"Maybe too well."

"Is there any way you can find out if Jackie Patnode is the older Lawrence girl? Could John Abbott tell us?"

"I don't think so. I have talked to him. He is very guarded when he answers my questions. I don't think he knows who Jackie Patnode is. I think he would have said something before now if he did."

"Maybe he doesn't know. Her appearance may have changed significantly in the last twenty years. Drugs do awful things to a person."

"My next step will be to try to get a DNA sample from Jackie. I will return to Jackie's apartment to see if I can find hairs on a hair-brush or something similar to use for DNA testing."

"Who will you compare her DNA to?"

"I would have to compare the DNA to a sample from the younger sister. I will have to contact her and see if she will be willing to provide a DNA sample for comparison."

That could open up a huge can of worms, Nell thought.

CHAPTER 72

Carrie has a lot to think about. She was irritated by the reprimand she had received at work from Rick and Nancy. Nancy had found the pearls that had been missing for several weeks in a draw that contained clothing accessories. "Really," Carrie had said, "both you and Jackie have to be more careful. These pearls are very valuable, and they could have been lost forever."

"I have put accessories in and out of the drawer several times in the last few weeks, and the pearls have not been in there," Carrie responded angrily as she left the office.

"Well, the pearls did not put themselves in there," Rick said sarcastically.

I wonder who put them in there, Carrie thought. *I have an idea who it might have been, but I have no idea why she would do such a thing. I am certainly not going to mention it to the Reardons, they would never believe me. Right now, I have other things to worry about.*

She could not quite understand why she had had this feeling of unease for the last few days. She had a sense that someone was following her, was present everywhere she went. Yet when she looked around, she never saw anyone.

She wondered if she should tell someone about this feeling. Certainly not Maggie, she did not want to worry her. She did not want to tell her Doug and Jane. They would worry and immediately feel they needed to visit her. Should she tell Scott or Chuck? Certainly not Chuck, he was just a casual date. Or was he? Should she contact Sgt. Tennyson from the police department? Maybe. *For now, I will just keep it to myself,* she decided.

When Carrie arrived home, her phone was ringing. She found herself hoping that it was Chuck who was calling. *Stop it,* she chided herself.

"Hello?"

"Carrie Franklin?" a man's voice asked.

"Yes."

"I have some information for you about your past. I will contact you again in a few days." The phone clicked.

Oh great, now a strange phone call. What is happening to me? Should I keep this to myself also?

The caller on the phone hoped she would talk to the correct person about the call.

CHAPTER 73

Pat Lawrence was surprised to see a policeman standing at her door. "Can I help you?" she asked.

"I am Sgt. Paul Tennyson from the Bellfield, Vermont, police department." Paul showed at his badge and department ID. "I would like to speak to you for a few moments, if I may.

Thank goodness Jenny is in school, this visit must not mean anything good, Pat thought as she stepped aside to allow Paul to enter the apartment. Paul explained the reason for his visit to Pat, then requested a DNA sample.

"I will of course supply the sample," Pat assured Paul, "but I don't really think it will be necessary. I can confirm that the person now known as Jackie Patnode is actually my sister, Donna Lawrence."

"How do you know that?"

"My eighteen-year-old daughter, against my wishes, has been visiting Bellfield, Vermont. She saw a picture in the window of a shop called the Unique Boutique. She brought a copy of the picture to me. I nearly died when I saw it."

"Why has your daughter been visiting Bellfield?"

"She found an old article about Rick Reardon in my desk. Apparently, I did not hide it well enough. When she asked me about the article I was, of course, evasive. She is a headstrong girl and decided to find out about this person herself."

"I assume she does not know about your relationship with the man in the picture."

"She does not, and must never find out."

"How did you find out that your sister is now called Jackie Patnode?"

"Again, from my daughter. She nosed around town and found out the names of the people in the picture. She was told that the woman in the picture was an employee of the Reardons, the other two people in the picture. She is very interested in the fact that the owner of the shop has the same name as the person in the newspaper article. Right now, she doesn't know any more than that."

"How long has it been since you have been in contact with your sister?"

"Over eighteen years. I assumed that she married her high school sweetheart and has kids in school by now."

"That is not the case." Paul told Pat what he knew about Jackie since her arrival in town to work at the boutique. and that she was now missing. He was not ready to divulge any information about event that occurred years ago.

"Where was she all those years before she started working at the boutique?"

"I am not sure. I was hoping you could provide that information."

"I am sorry, I can't."

"I would still like that DNA sample."

Pat willingly swabbed her cheek, and Paul carefully put the specimen in an evidence bag. He thanked Pat for her cooperation and went on his way.

CHAPTER 74

JOHN ABBOTT COULD NOT UNDERSTAND why someone would purchase the old house on Brook Street then just allow it to sit in disrepair. Also, he was nervous about the title search, which would have had to have been completed before the sale was finalized. What if the search revealed something about the child that was found there so many years ago? What if someone found out about his involvement? He did not want to question the Barkers about the sale. They would question his curiosity. He decided that his best move would be to drive by the house to see if any changes were being made. He could not quite understand the strange feeling he got every time he drove by the house. *It must be just because it is the house where the child was found all those many years ago,* he thought. He did not realize that his drive-bys were being carefully monitored.

As John was thinking about the house on Brook Street, Maude tapped quietly on his office door.

"Sgt. Tennyson is here to see you," she informed him.

Great, John thought, *that is all I need at this point.* John made sure that the door was tightly closed behind Paul after he came into the office. He knew Maude would be curious.

"John," Paul said as soon as the door was closed. "You need to stop playing games about the occurrences of twenty years ago.

"I know that you helped Nell hide the identity of the child found on Brook Street all those years ago. What you didn't know was that I was also involved in the decision to take the necessary steps to be sure no one would ever be able to locate her. The steps the three of us took may be questionable, but we felt the steps were necessary to ensure her safety."

John started to shake his head.

"Don't deny it, John. Facts are facts. You cannot deny your role in that situation.

"Also, you can no longer pretend that you know nothing about the young girl with whom Rick Reardon became involved. I know you were assisted by a church elder, Nell Warner's father, when working to solve the problem. Again, do not try to deny all this. I have spoken to both Nell and Pat Lawrence. What I don't know is whether Nell's cousin, Charles Warner, had anything to do with this."

John put his head in his hands. "Why are you digging up the past? The Lawrence girl, and as far as I know, her daughter, are living happy, healthy lives. Dredging up the past can have no purpose but to disrupt their lives. Why would anyone want to do that?"

"Before I answer that question, what can you tell me about the older sister in that family?"

"I can't tell you much. She stayed in town and had a child, but she never married. Her fiancé, the child's father, was killed in a military accident before the wedding could happen."

"Where is she now? Does she still live here in town?" Paul already knew the answer to that question. He wanted to know if John would be forthcoming.

"I have no idea," John stammered.

"Did she move with her family? If she moved out of town, where did she go?"

"I said I do not know."

"I don't know how a young woman and her young child can just disappear from a small town like Bellfield without someone questioning the move."

"Families move in and out of town all the time. It is their right."

"Was it convenient, John, to have this young woman leave town? Convenient that all the Lawrence family was out of town, out of sight, out of mind?"

"That suggestion is inexcusable, Paul."

"What is inexcusable, John, is that no one really cared what happened to the young woman and child. What is inexcusable is that the church members sighed a sigh of relief, and turned their back on them."

Paul then shocked John further by uttering Nell's exact words.

"I believe, John, that those two people have arrived back in town, but they did not arrive together."

John had forgotten about the window in his office that was slightly open. Maude had been able to listen to most of the conversation between John and Paul. She was in a panic. What would this mean to John's career? Would any of this information be made public? What did Paul mean about two people coming back to town? What two people? She needed to talk with someone about this. She made her regular phone call.

CHAPTER 75

Paul knew that it would be several weeks before he would receive the results from Pat Lawrence's DNA sample, but he was reasonably sure he had learned the true identity of Jackie Patnode. He was also certain that Jackie's disappearance was somehow related to her past. If, as he believed, Carrie Franklin was Jackie's daughter she might be in danger. He was not, however, ready to approach Carrie with his suspicions. And he was certainly not ready to alert the people of Bellfield of his findings. He was anxious to learn if the Reardons knew or were suspicious about Jackie's true identity. Paul did not have a picture of how Jackie looked twenty years ago, but he knew that her looks must have changed drastically. He was sure that John Abbott did not recognize her.

Oh no, now what? Rick Reardon groaned as he saw Paul walk into the store again.

"We need to talk," Paul told Rick and Nancy. "I don't believe your story about Jackie Patnode walking into your store seeking employment, and that you hired her on the spot. You did not even check for references."

"Well, it is true. We needed to fill the position, we liked what we saw, and we decided to give her a chance to prove herself. As it turns out, it was a good decision. Jackie has been an excellent employee."

Paul decided not to tell the Reardons what he believed to be Jackie's true identity. That could come later. He decided to try a veiled threat to see if he could get the true story about Jackie's employment.

"Rick, the statute of limitations for assault on a minor is twenty years. Your indiscretion was less than twenty years ago. You could still be charged for that unfortunate incident."

"I did not assault anyone."

"Well, the incident could certainly be considered an assault. The girl involved was under the age of consent."

Nancy, who until this point had been quiet during this conversation, said softly, "Rick, I think it is time we told the truth."

Rick sighed. "Charles Warner came into the boutique a few hours before Jackie arrived. He told Nancy and I that a young woman would be coming into the boutique applying for a job. He stated that he expected the girl to be hired if I did not want certain charges filed against me. He did not mention what the charges pertained to, but he knew I would understand what he was alluding to. We did not really believe charges would be filed but did not want to take a chance."

"As Rick said, Nancy stated, we have never regretted the decision. We have never had any problems with Jackie. She works hard, is reliable, and does excellent work."

"Thank you for finally telling me the true story of Jackie's employment. Why didn't you do that from the beginning?"

"Because Charles Warner told us not to."

That does not sound like the way Charles Warner would operate, Paul thought as he returned to his car. *I think I need to pay him a visit.*

Charles Warner was professional, but cool when he ushered Paul into his office.

"What can I do for you, Sergeant?"

"You can tell me what part you played to procure the employment of Jackie Patnode at the Unique Boutique several years ago."

"I played no part in that event."

"That is not what the Reardons told me."

"And just what did they tell you?"

"That you knew Jackie was going to apply for that position and that you threatened Rick with a sexual assault charge if she was not hired when she arrived at the boutique later that day."

"If I had made that call, which I doubt, it would have been on behalf of a client. Therefore, I would not be able to discuss it with you because of attorney/client privilege. Is there anything else I can do for you? I am late for a meeting."

As soon as Paul left his office, Charles made a phone call. "Paul Tennyson," he told the person on the other side of the line, "is asking about Jackie Patnode's arrival in town years ago, and her employment at the Unique Boutique. What do you purpose we do about it?"

Paul was deeply disturbed by Charles's attitude about his involvement in Jackie's employment years ago. He knew that Charles's son, Chuck, and Carrie Franklin were dating. Was that fact putting Carrie in danger?

CHAPTER 76

AFTER RECEIVING THE CALL FROM Maude Abbott, he realized that he could not wait any longer to put his plan into place. He had to work fast; a series of phone calls would cause a frenzy in Bellfield and in other places. The uproar would give him time to complete his plan. *I have to get the girl. No one must know about what I did to the girl years ago. I will be ruined.*

The first call was made to Pat Lawrence. Unfortunately, Jenny was also listening to the message as it played on the message machine. Both Jenny and Pat heard the caller say, "Mrs. Lawrence, when Sgt. Paul Tennyson from the Bellfield Police Department visited you, did he tell you that your sister was missing? I have her, and I don't believe she will be alive much longer. You may be able to help her if you tell the world who she really is."

"Mom," Jenny cried, "what is that person on the phone talking about? You don't have a sister."

Pat was shaking. "Sit down, Jenny. We need to talk. I need to tell you some things I was hoping you would never find out about. I don't know what is happening in Bellfield, Vermont, but occurrences there may affect us. I need to prepare you for any events that just may do that."

Jenny listened unbelievingly as Pat told her about her relationship with Rick Reardon when she was a very young girl. When she finished her story, she said, "Jenny you need to understand that what happened that fateful day was wrong, but I don't regret it because the result was you. I can't imagine a life without you."

"I have often wondered why you have lived such a lonely life and why you were always estranged from you parents. Now I guess I understand."

"I have not been lonely. I have you and my work. I have a lot of friends at work."

"What about the new man at your work, David Donovan? He seems to be interested in you."

"David is the first man I have met over the years that I thought I might be interested in. But I can never develop a serious relationship with anyone. I don't want anyone to know about my past, and I can't develop a relationship that is not based on complete honesty."

"When I learned I was expecting you, I placed my hand on my stomach and promised you would have a happy childhood. That has been my life's mission. Nothing else was important."

"And I have. No one could ask for a better mom than you. Now we need to think about you, not just me. We need to find out what is going on in Bellfield."

"No, we don't, Jenny. Neither of us is ever going to go to Bellfield again. There is a policeman there who is searching for my sister. We must hope he will find her safe and sound. We need to leave it at that."

We will see, Jenny thought.

CHAPTER 77

CHUCK WARNER COULD TELL THAT his father was distracted, that he had something on his mind that he had not shared with either him or his mother.

"What gives, Dad, what is troubling you?" he asked.

Charles decided to be truthful. "Many years ago, I did something to help my cousin Nell that might not have been quite kosher. It may come back now to haunt me."

"What did you do?"

"I just made a phone call."

"Come on, Dad, come clean. Who did you make the call to, and why did you make it?"

"Call your mother in. You both may as well know about this." Once his wife and son were settled down in chairs, Charles began to talk.

"Many years ago, a young child was found on the steps of that old house on Brook Street. Paul Tennyson was called to the scene. It appeared that the child had been abused, and Nell was called in to place the child in a safe environment. When Paul returned to the house to continue his investigation, he found a young woman inside badly doped up. She was in such tough shape that she had no recollection of who she was or how she got into the house. She could not recall anything about her past. Both Nell and Paul believed both the woman and the child were in grave danger. With the help of John Abbott, they expunged all evidence of their existence. The woman was placed in a drug-rehabilitation center, and the child was placed in foster care out of town. I helped with some of the arrangements, that is all."

"No, Dad, I don't believe that is all, Tell us the rest."

"A few years ago, the young woman was ready to be released from the rehabilitation center she had been living ever since she was found here in town. She had no past. She did not know who she was. She needed a job and a place to live. The center called John for assistance because he had been instrumental in placing her with them. It was up to him to find the young woman a job and a place to call home.

"He knew there was a job opening at the Unique Boutique. He also knew the Reardons were having difficulty filling the position because of an indiscretion in Rick's past. He wanted to be sure the young woman got that job and enlisted my help

"I am not proud of what I did, but I wanted to help John and Nell. Nell was still very worried about the woman's safety. Charles told Joan and Chuck about the phone call he made to Rick. It could be construed as a threatening phone call."

"What happened to the young woman?" Chuck asked.

"Right now, we don't know," Charles answered. "The woman was given the name of Jackie Patnode."

"Oh my god," Chuck and Joan said in unison.

CHAPTER 78

CARRIE DECIDED NOT TO ANSWER her phone when it rang shortly after she returned home from the boutique. She had been receiving too many calls with upsetting messages as well as hung-up calls. *Someone is trying to frighten me,* she thought, *and they are doing a pretty good job.*

After the phone's leave-a-message announcement, Carrie heard Chuck's voice.

"Carrie, it's Chuck. Call me…"

"I'm here, Chuck," Carrie said.

"Are you screening your calls?"

Carrie decided to tell Chuck about the feelings of unease she had been experiencing lately, and about the strange calls she had been getting.

"For the past few days, I have been having the feeling that I am being watched. It doesn't make sense, because when I look around, I don't see anyone. About a week ago I received a call from some man who said he had some information about my past and would get back to me. I have not heard from him since. To make matters worse, I have received several calls from someone who hangs up as soon as I say hello. Sometimes a voice says, 'You are in danger' then hangs up. Anyway, that is why I did not answer the phone when you called."

"What are you doing for dinner tonight?"

"I don't know. I haven't given it a thought."

"I will pick up a pizza and wine and will be right over."

"That is great!" Carrie was excited about seeing Chuck tonight.

After calling in for the pizza, Chuck spoke to his parents about his concern for Carrie.

"Do you think I should tell Carrie what we expect about Jackie Patnode?"

"Why would you do that?"

"I think there might be a connection between Jackie's disappearance and the phone calls Carrie is getting."

"I think so too," Charles said. "I was afraid to verbalize the thought."

"I have also been thinking about those two," Joan said softly. "I wonder if Carrie is Jackie's child."

Both men were shocked at this revelation.

"Why do you think that, Joan?" Charles asked.

"I think the fact that both have come here to this town is more than a coincidence."

Charles agreed. "I do too. I am suspicious of the fact that neither woman has any history prior to their arrival in Bellfield. I guess John, Nell, and I did our job very well. There is no way that that child from Brook Street could find any connection to Bellfield. I think Carrie Franklin's background is still a mystery."

Charles hoped his family would buy his story.

Chuck was relieved.

CHAPTER 79

Nancy Reardon was surprised to see the young girl enter the boutique. The merchandise on display at the shop was designed to appeal to women in their early twenties or older. It was not something a young girl would be interested in purchasing for herself. *Perhaps she is looking for something for her mother or another relative,* Nancy thought, *and I hope she is aware of our price ranges. She does not appear to be someone with a lot of money to spend.*

"Can I help you?" Nancy asked the young girl.

Jenny was beginning to lose her courage, but she said timidly, "I came here to meet my dad."

"I think you might be in the wrong place," Nancy replied. "There is no one here who has a child. Do you want to tell me who you are looking for? Perhaps I can head you in the right direction. I know most of the people who live in Bellfield."

Jenny spoke the name that Nancy was hoping not to hear.

"My name is Jenny Lawrence. I am looking for someone named Rick Reardon."

Nancy tried to hide how shaken she was. She spoke in a very businesslike manner.

"Come with me to the office. I will introduce you to Mr. Reardon."

After making the introductions, Nancy fled to the restroom. She washed her face in cold water, then leaned against the wall to steady herself. She had wanted to put the "closed" sign on the shop's door, so she wouldn't have to see anyone for a few moments, but she expected Carrie to return from her lunch break at any time. Carrie would question the "closed" sign.

Nancy's thoughts were a jumbled mess.

Rick and Pat Lawrence had produced a beautiful child.

Why had she not been able to have a child? *Because I have been so cold to Rick all these years,* she thought. *It takes certain activities to have a child.*

Why couldn't I have accepted what happened and forgiven Rick?

We could have gone on to have a happy marriage.

Lord knows I still love the guy. I believe he still loves me.

What on earth am I going to do now?

Nancy heard the bell on the door ring, indicating she had a customer. She knew Carrie had not yet returned from lunch. She quickly powdered her nose, smoothed her dress, patted her hair into place, put on a smile, and went out into the store to greet her customer, trying to ignore the two people she could see talking earnestly through the office window.

As soon as Nancy closed the office door, Jenny plopped down in one of the chairs and asked, "Why did you deny that you were Rick Reardon when I was here before?"

"I had no idea who you were or what you wanted. Businesspeople have to be careful about the kind of information they give out to strangers."

"That is a lousy excuse."

"It is not an excuse, it is a reason."

"Did you love my mother?"

"No, and she did not love me. What happened was an inappropriate response to a tender moment. Many people have suffered for that mistake. Everyone involved was determined that only adults suffered though admittedly your mother was not quite an adult at the time. She was considered to be one. All of us wanted to be sure that you would never suffer for our mistakes. I believe you have lived a comfortable, happy life."

"I have."

"Does your mother know you are here?"

"No, my mother said that neither of us should ever come to Bellfield again."

"And your mother was right. Jenny, your curiosity and events here in Bellfield have made it necessary for your mother and me to contact each other for the first time in twenty years. Both you and your mother have my phone number. If either of you ever need anything, anything at all, contact me and I will help in any way I can. That is all the support I can give you."

"My mom told me," Jenny said quietly, "that my dad died before I was born. That was a lie. She also told me that my dad was a good man. Maybe that was not a lie."

Jenny left the office and the store.

CHAPTER 80

"Carrie," Chuck said as they munched pizza and sipped wine, "what are your plans for the future? I am sure you do not want to spend your life working for the Reardons at the Unique Boutique."

"I hope to return to school someday and study to be a pediatric nurse, but first I have to find out who I am, and I have to learn to banish my fears. I see Scott Wynters once a week, and he is helping me solve those issues. I hope someday to be able to develop a strong relationship with someone, maybe even marry and have a family."

"I think you know I hope that someone will be me."

"I hope that also, but I have a long way to go." This was the first time Carrie had allowed herself to think of Chuck in this way. She was surprised that she verbalized it to Chuck. She went on hurriedly, "All this will take a very long time."

"I am a very patient man."

"Scott is trying very hard to help me resolve all my demons, but things are progressing very slowly. He wants me to undergo hypnosis, but I don't think I am ready for that.

"Then don't do it. You will know when the time is right."

Carrie was gratified by the fact that Chuck was not going to try to push her into something she was not ready for. *He really understands me*, she thought.

"Is Scott trying to help you understand why you have such strong feelings about the house on Brook Street, and why you feel you have been at the playground we talked about recently?" Chuck was thinking about the differing opinions his mother and father have about who Carrie actually was. He asked the question very cautiously.

"Scott believes I may have lived here in Bellfield when I was a very young child."

For lord's sake, Chuck thought to himself, *do the darn hypnosis.* He knew better than to say that aloud.

"Do you believe that too?"

"I just don't know what to believe."

"Scott is also helping me with another problem. He is attempting to help me understand my adverseness to being touched. He thinks I may have hurt when I was a very young child, and as a result I am not able to trust any adult who shows me affection by touching me."

The more Chuck heard Carrie talk, the more he believed she may be the child who was found on the steps of the house on Brook Street. He still doubted there was any relationship between Carrie and Jackie Patnode.

"I hope someday you will allow me to help you with that problem."

"Tell me about the feeling you have that you are being watched."

"I don't know if I would say that I have the feeling that I am being watched. It is more like I have the feeling that someone is around me all the time."

"Have you discussed this with Scott?"

"I have. He thinks it is because I am developing the feeling that I have been here before, that I know some of the people here. He also says I need to be aware of my surroundings at all times, and that I should not be out alone at night."

"I'll second that. Tell me about the phone calls again."

"There isn't much to tell. Just that someone hangs up as soon as I answer. Sometimes I know there is someone on the line, but they don't speak. At those times, I just hang up."

"Do you have caller ID?"

"I do."

"Great, if you don't recognize the caller, don't answer at all."

"What if the person calls that says he knows something about my past?"

"If the person is legitimate, he will find a more appropriate way to contact you."

Just then the phone rang. "May I pick it up?" Chuck asked.

Carrie nodded.

"Franklin residence." Chuck heard a click.

Why is a man answering her phone? he thought angrily? *She is mine.*

CHAPTER 81

PAUL WAS SURPRISED THAT THE results from the DNA samples from Pat Lawrence and Jackie Patnode's hairbrush came back as quickly as they did. *I guess it pays to have clout,* he thought. Police Chief Jacobs had put a request in to the lab to prioritize these samples, and send the results as quickly as possible.

Paul knocked on the chief's office door and was given permission to enter the office.

"Thanks for putting a rush on these DNA samples."

"The timing was good. We sent in the samples at a time that the lab was not awfully busy."

"What did the results show?"

"The DNA samples were a match for siblings. It appears that Pat Lawrence and Jackie Patnode are sisters. Jackie Patnode is, in reality, Donna Lawrence. Quite frankly, I was very surprised at this revelation. No way did I acquaint Jackie Patnode with the shriveled-up woman I found in that house on Brook Street nearly twenty years ago, and I did not know Donna Lawrence."

"I am surprised that people such as John Abbott and Rick Reardon did not recognize her."

"I suspect they did. It appeared that at the time we found her, that the drugs in her system were administered to her were not self-inflicted. Someone wanted to do her a great deal of harm. That is the reason why we went to such great lengths to hide her identity. We did not know who her assailant was, and did not want him or her to ever be able to locate her."

"It now appears that person has, in fact, found her. Have you searched the house on Brook Street?"

"No, there is no reason to. The house was recently purchased by Michael Abbott, John's brother. He is now in the process of securing funding to rehabilitate the house. He wants, eventually, to use the property as a drug-rehabilitation center."

"How did you learn that?"

"I ran into Ben Barker the other day at lunch. He is contemplating asking some civic club to run a fundraiser for the cause."

"That is probably a good idea. The drug problem among teens in this town is accelerating."

"Back to the original subject. How do you purpose to continue searching for Jackie Patnode, short of searching every building in this town?"

"I guess by talking to everyone again to see what they can recall about the last time they remember seeing her before her disappearance."

"I plan to set up a task force to search all abandoned buildings in town. It may be a waste of time and man power, but I do not want to leave any stone unturned. We may eventually want to attempt to get a warrant to search the house on Brook Street. That may be difficult to do."

Paul knew it was right to first notify the chief of police of the results of the DNA samples. The second person he wanted to talk to was Nell Warner.

Nell was shocked to learn that Jackie Patnode was in reality Donna Lawrence. "Are you absolutely sure?" she asked Paul.

"That is what the DNA test results tell us."

"I never saw the young woman you found on Brook Street. My job was to assist the little girl that was found the same day, and I never knew Donna Lawrence. My father said she just up and moved out of the area."

"Didn't anyone ever check to see where she went? What about her clothes, furniture, etc.? Someone must have seen a moving van or something."

"I agree. Quite frankly, I think the town ignored the situation because having Jackie, or rather Donna Lawrence, leave town would help the scandal about her sister and Rick Reardon go away. Out of sight, out of mind. Do you want me to talk to my father again?"

"No, let's talk to John first."

John pretended to be shocked when Paul and Nell told him that Jackie Patnode was, in reality, Donna Lawrence. "Come on, John," Paul said. "I think both you and Charles Warner knew who Jackie really was when you asked Charles to make that somewhat threatening phone call to Rick encouraging him to hire her to work at the Unique Boutique."

"No," John said. "Charles did not know who she was, and I didn't either until I saw her. We took the drastic step to appease the rehab center. They stated that Jackie has to be discharged and that she needed to find employment and a place to live before that could happen. I prevailed upon Charles to help me, and he did so, with some reservations, just to assist me in a solving a difficult situation.

"Twenty years ago, two events occurred in town at about the same time. One was finding a woman we could not identify who desperately needed help. I did not realize that the two events were connected, but now I believe they were.

"I was contacted by church members. Nell's father was one, and was told that Donna Lawrence and her young child had left town to live with a friend. I got the idea that it was a male friend, but didn't really know. I was asked to have a mover go to Donna's apartment and move her belongings to a storage facility. I was told it would be best if it was done at night. Of course, I was not completely comfortable with doing this, but I complied. I believe some ladies from the church cleaned the apartment when everything was moved. The apartment was later rented to another family. I often wondered where the mother and child were, but assumed they were well and happy."

"A few days later I was called by the hospital and asked for assistance in placing a young woman from town, but not necessarily a parishioner, into a drug-rehabilitation center. I made the arrangements, and the young woman was transported by ambulance from the hospital to the rehab center. I had no idea who the patient was.

"Nell and I were responsible for that phone call. Neither of us knew who the patient was either. We just wanted to be sure that whoever wanted to hurt her would never be able to find her. We called you because we knew, as a pastor, that you would never discuss what happened."

"And I never have until this moment." John did not tell Nell and Paul about Michael.

"By the way, Donna's things are no longer in storage. I am not at liberty to tell you what happened to them. Everything that happened in the past is past. What we need to do now is to find Jackie—er… Donna—before someone hurts her again. How do you purpose doing that, Paul?"

"Chief Jacobs is organizing a search party to look through all vacant buildings, woods, etc. But I don't think she will be found that way. I think someone has her confined somewhere. They may not still be in Bellfield."

"A search of empty factories in this town will take a while," John said bitterly. He could recall days when he was a child when Bellfield was a thriving industrial town.

"We need to put our heads together and think of everyone we can who was connected to Donna Lawrence all those years ago. Maybe we can come up with the names of people who potentially would want to cause her harm."

John recalled that his brother Michael was smitten with both Pat and Donna when they were very young, but did not mention his name. He knew his brother would not have anything to do with Jackie's disappearance.

CHAPTER 82

Chuck and his dad were having a similar conversation; only, their concern was about Carrie, not Jackie.

"Dad, I have been racking my brain about who might want to scare, or even worse, hurt Carrie, but I just can't come up with anything."

"Why don't you call the Waters to see if they have any insight into the matter? Something happened to connect Carrie with Bellfield. Just try not to alarm them. Ensure them that we are watching over her."

Doug Waters listened carefully as Chuck told him about Carrie's feelings of unease about the hang-up calls and about the call Carrie received from someone claiming that they had information about her past and would call her at a later date and share the information.

"I am watching over her as is Sgt. Paul Tennyson. I told her not to meet with anyone alone, that I would go with her, or if she preferred, she could ask her counselor, Scott Wynters, to accompany her."

"Thank you for that. I think Jane and I will drive down for a visit this weekend."

"Good Idea. In the meantime, will you see if you can come up with anything that will help us learn something about her past?"

"Jane and I have thought and thought about that. The only thing we can come up with is the phone number with Bellfield's area code. It may be significant because the paper with the number on it was quickly removed from our sight by the case worker who brought Carrie in. She seemed stressed that she had inadvertently let us see it. Also, Jane thinks she has heard the name Maggie Scranton, but that probably is a minor issue."

That is not minor, Chuck thought. *It could be huge.*

As soon as he was done talking with Doug Waters, Chuck called Nell. "How could Jane Waters know about Maggie Scranton?" he asked her.

Nell was sure that Chuck, or anyone else for that matter, did not know that Maggie had found an injured child on Brook Street. Maggie had promised not to reveal that fact to anyone, and Nell was sure Maggie had kept her promise. Except for that one occurrence, Maggie was just a nondescript, small-town lady. That would not be true if people knew about her finding a child.

"Nell, I am going to start looking quietly into the backgrounds of influential people in this town. If Carrie is from here, someone must know something."

"Just be careful, Chuck."

Chuck's research found nothing that raised a red flag. Most of the residents of Bellfield were upstanding citizens who had lived in the town all their lives. Young families who moved in would not have had anything to do with events that occurred years ago. The one exception was Michael Abbott, John's brother who had moved out of town, then moved back recently.

He learned that there was one eccentric resident of Bellfield. Ms. Emily Prudhomme was a spinster who lived in the once-abandoned house on Brook Street with her parents and remained in the house with her cats after her parents died. When she died, she left the house to any kin who would be willing to move into the house and care for the cats. Apparently, that person was never found. The cats were adopted out, and the house was left in disrepair.

Chuck wondered how the house was finally able to be placed on the market. He called Ben Barker about the issue.

"I received a notarized letter from a Ms. Anita Prudhomme," Ben explained. "Ms. Prudhomme authorized the sale of the house with the stipulation that the proceeds from the sale be placed in a trust under her name until she returns to this country. She is currently living in England.

"A title search determined that the Prudhommes were the sole owners of the property. That fact legitimized the sale, and the house was placed on the market. It was purchased by an out-of-town corporation. I understand that they want to eventually use the home as a drug-rehabilitation center."

After he hung up the phone, Ben realized he had forgotten to tell Chuck that Michael Abbott was the executor of the Prudhomme estate. Oh well, I will tell him the next time I speak with him, Ben thought.

CHAPTER 83

THE INFORMATION THAT MAUDE HAD been sharing with him for the last few months was invaluable, but now it was time for him to act. Maude had outlived her usefulness. He did not wish to communicate with her any longer. He had to be sure she would never divulge what she had done, but how? Another disappearance was not the answer; it would be too suspect. He could attempt to scare her into silence, but that method was too risky. Maude liked to talk too much. He devised a plan.

It was Jim Felton's last night to work at the Star Restaurant as a busboy. It was on to college for him. When he was asked to do a favor for the gentleman, he hesitated. However, when he was offered a fifty-dollar bill as a tip, he complied to the request—he needed the money. Delivering a bottle of wine to a lady seemed harmless enough.

He approached the table where the ladies from the town were enjoying their monthly luncheon. He handed the bottle of wine to Maude, saying, "Compliments from a gentleman who wishes to remain anonymous."

At first, the ladies were stunned by this unusual event, then Maggie, Emma, Nora, and Jane Croteau started to laugh and clap. "Maude," said Emma, "a gift of wine from an anonymous admirer. What will John think?"

"Read the note that is attached," Nora requested.

"Enjoy this bottle of wine at home," Maude read. "Thank you for being such an excellent pastor's wife." It was signed "An appreciative church member."

Maude did not read the last sentence of the note that stated, "Your discretion will be appreciated, actually demanded, and necessary for your health."

Maude tried to act nonchalant as her friend's good-natured teasing continued, but she was frightened. She knew the last sentence was a threat. She did not want John to ever find out about the phone calls she had made even though she believed with all her heart that they were for his protection. She would keep her counsel.

She did not know what information her coconspirator had that could hurt John, but he had assured her that he had evidence that John had made a terrible mistake many years ago that could cost him his position as pastor of the church. Her partner in crime had promised that the information she provided him would be used only to protect John if it became necessary.

Protection for John was all Maude wanted.

CHAPTER 84

Carrie knew that Chuck, and for that matter, Scott, would be unhappy that she was meeting with her caller on her own. She was, however, comfortable with the meeting. After all, she knew him, often saw him at church socials. She had called both Chuck and Scott to see if they wanted to go to the mall with her, but Chuck had a dinner meeting with a client, and Scott was seeing a patient.

He greeted her politely as they sat down outside Starbucks. He asked her if she would like something to eat or drink.

"A cup of coffee would be great."

"I will join you in a coffee. I'll get them, then we can talk."

When he left the table to get the coffee, Carrie noticed a manila folder on the chair beside her. She assumed it held information about her past.

When he returned with the coffee, he said, "Carrie, I am going to tell you who your real parents are. You may be quite surprised. Your father was a resident of this town who died in a military accident before you were born. You know your mother quite well."

Carrie was trying to listen to what he was saying. He was saying something about a family with the last name of Lawrence who lived in Bellfield many years ago. What he was saying was not registering. She was having a difficult time concentrating, and was beginning to feel quite nauseated. She started looking around for a restroom sign.

Carrie interrupted the speaker by saying, "I am very anxious to hear what you have to tell me, but for some reason, I am feeling very ill. I think I need to go home. Can we arrange another meeting?"

"Of course, we can. I will call you when you feel better. Let me walk you to your car. Are you all right to drive?"

"Yes, I am fine to drive. My head is clear, and I have a very short trip home."

They walked out of the mall and headed for Carrie's car. He was holding her by the elbow. Carrie suddenly felt a sharp prick, then remembered nothing.

Maggie had been a little concerned when she retired for the evening and Carrie was not yet home. When she got up at midnight to get a drink of water, she checked to see if Carrie's car was in the garage. The window in her kitchen allowed her to see through the windows of the garage. Carrie's car was not there. She thought about calling Sgt. Tennyson, then admonished herself. *Don't be such a busy-body*, she thought. *Carrie is an attractive young woman. She has the right to be out all night if she wants to without her landlady checking on her. I hope she is with Chuck Warner. He seems like a very nice young man.*

When Maggie awoke around seven the next morning, she checked again to see if Carrie's car was in the garage. She would know then that everything was all right. The car was not there. This worried her greatly.

What should I do? she wondered. *I don't want to make a mountain out of a molehill, don't want to interfere with a lover's tryst if that is what is going on. The trouble is, this is not at all like Carrie. I think I will call Joan Warner.*

"Mrs. Warner," she said when the ring was answered, "this is Maggie Scranton. I am sorry to bother you, but I am worried about Carrie Franklin. Do you know if she was with Chuck last night?

"I don't believe she was. He had a late dinner meeting with a client. Why do you ask?"

"She went out last night about six and never returned home. That is not like her."

Charles and Chuck were sitting at the breakfast table listening to Joan's side of the conversation.

"What do you mean she never returned home?"

Charles and Chuck were becoming alarmed.

"I never saw any lights in her apartment last night, and her car is not in the garage."

"Maggie, I will give this information to my husband and son. Hang in there, someone will be right over."

When Chuck heard the news from his mother, he asked her to cancel all his appointments for the day. He headed over to Carrie's apartment.

CHAPTER 85

MAGGIE WAS RELIEVED TO SEE Chuck drive into her driveway. "I hope I am not bothering you for no reason," Maggie stated.

"No, you are not. I appreciate the phone call. We need to get to the bottom of this."

"Have you contacted Carrie's parents?"

"Not yet. I don't want to alarm them. I will call them as soon as I have anything to tell them. Do you know where Carrie was headed when she went out last night?"

"She said she was meeting someone at the mall."

That sent up a red flag for Chuck. He was careful not to let Maggie know he was alarmed.

"I am going to drive over to the mall to see if anyone remembers seeing her there last night. I will get back to you soon."

Chuck was not in the parking lot long before he spotted Carrie's car near the main entrance. He immediately called Paul Tennyson. He decided to walk through the main parts of the mall to see if Carrie was there while he waited for Paul to arrive. He did not really expect to find Carrie there and soon returned to where her car was parked. He walked around the car and looked, as well as he could, through the windows. He knew better than to touch anything.

When Paul arrived he also walked carefully around the car, bent down, and looked under the car, finding nothing of interest. He also looked through the windows, taking care not to touch the glass.

"Tell me again what Maggie said about Carrie's movements last night."

Chuck told him everything he knew.

"I would like to tow Carrie's car and have it searched, but I have no probable cause." She could have met a friend and gone somewhere with him or her, leaving her car here until they return.

Chuck did not appreciate the pronoun *him*.

"Do you have a picture of Carrie?"

"I don't, and I don't think anyone here in town would have one. Of course, her parents would."

"Call them and see if they would fax a picture to me. Once I receive it, I will show it to people who worked here at the mall last night. Maybe someone will remember seeing her."

Chuck called the Waters and explained the situation to them. They immediately faxed a picture of Carrie to Paul, then packed clothes and headed for Bellfield.

CHAPTER 86

Maggie had encouraged Doug and Jane to stay at Carrie's apartment while they remained in town. "It is what Carrie would want you to do," she explained.

"Okay," Jane said, "we will stay for now, but when Carrie comes home, we will move to the Motel 6. This apartment is too small for three people."

Even too small for two people, Doug thought.

Chuck called Paul as soon as Doug and Jane arrived in town.

"Do you think we should get together and brainstorm? Maybe as a group we could come up with something that will help us understand what is happening with Carrie."

"I do. Do you think we should contact Scott and Nan Wynters? Carrie has become close friends with Nan, and she has therapy sessions every week with Scott."

"Maybe we could meet for dinner," Chuck suggested.

When Scott was contacted, he suggested that they meet at his home. He did not think that meeting in a public place was a good idea. Doug and Jane insisted on bringing pizza and wine to Scott's home. The pair did not want Nan to have to cook for them.

"I can only stay for a few minutes," Paul explained. "My son is playing in a soccer tournament, and I need to be there. My wife has been very understanding about the long hours I have been working, but I know both she and my son would be very disappointed if I missed the game. I won't do that to them, and I want very much to be there."

When Paul said his wife was very understanding, Scott smiled at Nan lovingly. "Sounds like my wife," he said to no one in particular.

Paul continued. "As soon as I received Carrie's picture from her parents, I showed it to several people, who were working at the mall last night. A barrister at Starbucks thought she saw Carrie sitting at one of the tables outside the store, but she wasn't sure. They were very busy, and she did not know if Carrie was with someone, or if she was alone. She did not believe Carrie was there for very long.

"I need to go, but before I do, I want to leave you with a suggestion as to how to proceed with your conversation. Start at the very beginning. Start with what Doug and Jane know about the phone number Jane noticed many years ago. Jane, think very hard about why the name Maggie Scranton seems similar to you."

Jane spoke up after Paul said his goodbyes. "When the social worker arrived at our home with Carrie, she brought papers that needed to be signed. I saw the phone number on a paper she brought with her, but did not give to us to sign. Maybe the name Maggie Scranton was on that paper. I have no idea."

Scott turned to Jane. "Has Carrie ever said anything to you about a house that she may remember, or about playing at a playground when she was a very young child?"

"No, Carrie said very little when she first came to us. She always seemed fearful and distrustful."

"I strongly believe," Scott said, "that Carrie had some ties to this community when she was very young. I also believe that something traumatic happened to her here in Bellfield. That event may have occurred at the house on Brook Street."

Something about the house on Brook Street hopped onto Chuck's mind, but he instantly lost it.

"Carrie told me she believes she has ties to Brook Street," Nan said quietly, "however, she is totally confused about why she feels that way."

"Why do you believe that?" Doug asked Scott.

"I am a little concerned about breaking client/counselor confidentiality. However, under the circumstances, I feel I must speak. I hope Carrie will understand. I am sure you have all recognized Carrie's reluctance to allow anyone to touch her. I am positive that is a symptom of something that happened to her when she was very young. What that was, I have no idea. She is working hard to change that behavior, working hard to trust people. She is making progress in that area. Jane and Doug, I am happy with the reports that Carrie allows you to pat her hand, touch her shoulder, etc. The progress she has made with Doug is exceptional."

Thank the Lord, Chick sighed inwardly.

"I have taken Carrie to the house on Brook Street. With me by her side, she is now able to walk up the walk to the steps. I don't believe she is ready to do this on her own."

"The first time we started up the sidewalk," she said in the tiniest voice.

"Do not hurt baby."

"I don't think she realized she said that, and I did not mention it to her."

"Oh lord," Jane cried, "what could have happened to her there?" Tears filled her eyes. Doug put his arm around his wife.

While Jane was wondering what had happened to Carrie years ago, Carrie was wondering what was happening to her now. She felt ill, hurt all over, and couldn't think. She was aware that someone was in the room with her, but she did not know who it was. Her eyes were blurry, preventing her from seeing well.

All of a sudden, she heard a familiar voice say, "Oh god, Carrie, what has he done to you?"

CHAPTER 87

CHUCK WAS DISCOURAGED. AFTER HE, Scott, Nan, Doug, and Jane talked for about two hours they had to admit they were not able to come up with any definitive answers as to why Carrie was gone. He talked to Charles the next morning.

"Maybe you need to delve further into the history of the property on Brook Street," Charles advised. "Call Ben Barker again and see if he can give you any more information about how the Prudhomme estate was settled. Then see if you can settle down and work. We have a lot of active files that need to be taken care of."

"Good idea."

"Ben is out of town for a couple of days," Barb informed Chuck when he called the real estate office. "I will have him call you when he returns."

Chuck spent the rest of the morning trying to do what his father asked, but he simply could not concentrate on the cases he was trying to review. He knocked on his dad's office door and walked in.

"It is useless. I can't concentrate. I am going to call Barb Barker again and get a phone number for Ben. I know Carrie's disappearance has to do with her past. She is somehow connected negatively to the house on Brook Street. Her minor memories of the playground are happy ones, so I doubt her disappearance is connected to any other part of her life in Bellfield."

"Go ahead," said Charles. "First give me your most pressing files. I will see what I can do to help you with them."

Barb Barker was irritated when Chuck called again. "Ben is at an important real estate meeting. I don't want him disturbed."

"Mrs. Barker, two people from Bellfield are missing. Ben may unwittingly have information that will help us locate them."

Barb sighed. "I will give you Ben's hotel information and cell phone number."

"Thank you. I really appreciate your help."

Ben was a little irritated when his cell phone rang, and Chuck's name came up on the caller ID. He had told Barb not to give out his phone number.

"Chuck, this call better be important. I am in the middle of a meeting with several potential clients."

"Carrie Franklin is missing," Chuck informed Ben. "Sgt. Tennyson, Carrie's parents, myself, and others believe her disappearance is somehow connected to the property on Brook Street that you recently sold. I was hoping that you may have remembered some information about that property that you did not recall when we talked earlier. Anything might be helpful."

Ben's tone softened. "I am sorry to hear about Carrie. I hope she is found safe and sound. I don't think I have any more information about the Prudhomme property. I believe I did forget to mention that Michael Abbott was the executor of the Prudhomme estate."

"Thank you, Ben."

I don't think that information will lead me anywhere, Chuck thought. *I will talk to Dad again.*

"Dad, do you have any idea why Michael Abbott, John's brother, would be the executor of the Prudhomme estate?"

"Prudhomme?"

"They are the last people to have owned the Brook Street property. In fact, I believe they were the sole owners. When the last family member died, she left the property to distant relatives under the condition that they live at the property and care for her cats. No one bit, so the house has been left unoccupied."

"Someone has to be paying taxes, buying fuel so the pipes won't freeze, etc."

"I will talk to John."

Chuck called Paul and gave him what little information he had gleaned then headed for the rectory.

CHAPTER 88

John Abbott was not in a good mood. He was trying to write the sermon for his Sunday service.

It was not going well, and he had had several interruptions. He was not happy when Maude told him that Chuck Warner wanted to speak with him.

"What can I do for you, Chuck?" John tried to sound cordial, but his irritation showed through.

"John, I need to learn all I can about the abandoned property on Brook Street."

"I know nothing about that property."

"Ben Barker said you were interested in purchasing that property."

"It was just a foolish moneymaking whim. I was fortunate that someone purchased it before I did. I would have probably lost a lot of money."

Maude, who of course was listening, was gratified to hear John make that concession.

"What is your relationship with the Prudhommes, the former owners?"

"I have no relationship with that family. I don't believe I even know them."

"Then why was your brother, Michael, the executor of the Prudhomme estate?"

"I didn't know he was."

Maude broke into the room. She shook a finger at Chuck and said, "Michael was not the executor of the estate. John was. He accidentally"—Maude put her hands in the air, making what looked like quotation marks around the word *accidentally*—"put the funds from the sale of the property into an account that was not the Prudhommes' account. I demand that you drop this investigation immediately. If you don't, you will ruin my husband's career, his very life."

CHAPTER 89

HE WAS NOT HAPPY WITH the phone call he had just received. He needed to decide quickly what his next move would be. He watched through the basement window to see how his captives were faring.

The two women were not aware that they were being watched. He had lowered the amount of drugs he had been administering to them, so they would be able to communicate. He wanted to see if they would reestablish the bond they had developed while working together at the boutique. He could not hear what they were saying, but he could read their body language. He had a sense that they were establishing a friendship. *They are probably wondering how they can save themselves*, he thought, *but any attempt will be futile. I haven't decided if I will reveal their past to them before their end comes.*

Carrie had been surprised when she heard someone speak her name. Now she realized that the other person in the room with her was Jackie Patnode.

"I am beginning to feel a little better, Jackie. Are you?"

"Yes, it is because he is playing games with us. He is giving us less drugs so we can think more clearly, though I don't understand why."

Then Jackie broke into tears. "I worked so hard to get clean when I was at the rehab center. Now I will never be clean again."

"Yes, you will. You did it before and you can do it again. How did you get into the drugs before? Did it start with legal prescription drugs?"

"I have no idea. I can't remember anything about my life before waking up at the center. The doctors say I have drug-induced amnesia. They say I may recall some of my past eventually, but it has not happened yet."

Maybe Scott will be able to help Jackie after we get out of here, Carrie thought.

"I don't know why we are being kept here," Carrie told Jackie, "but I am sure the reasons are nefarious. We need to devise a plan to get out of here. Do you know how long you have been confined here?"

"I am not sure. Maybe about a week."

"Jackie, everyone in town is very worried about you. Sgt. Paul Tennyson has been searching for you for several days. Maybe he is searching for me too. I know Chuck Warner will look for me also."

"I hope they will find us in time," Jackie said.

Carrie was surprised by this comment. It had not occurred to her before that she would not get out of this situation safely.

"We will be fine," she said quickly. "He is bringing us food and water."

"And he is drugging us."

"Maybe he is holding us for ransom."

"No one is going to pay a ransom for me," Jackie told Carrie. "I have no family." When Jackie made this comment, a picture of some people flashed in her mind. She quickly dismissed the image.

I think Doug and Jane would pay a ransom for me, Carrie thought. Maybe Chuck would also. She did not verbalize these thoughts to Jackie.

CHAPTER 90

"HAS OUR INVESTIGATOR FOUND ANYTHING useful?" Chuck asked his dad hopefully.

"Unfortunately, there is nothing all that new. He confirmed what John had already told us. Apparently, John is acquainted with a computer whiz who lives in southern New Hampshire who has the knowledge necessary to expunge information such as dates of birth, social security numbers, anything to prove a person existed at some time from data bases. At the request of Paul and Nell, he contacted that person and asked to have information about Donna Lawrence, who we know as Jackie Patnode, expunged. He also requested that the young child be given a fake identity. This work was also completed. This was a drastic act, but all felt it necessary to protect the woman and child."

"This computer person sounds like a shady character."

"I don't know if he is. Few people know his identity. Obviously, his clientele are very protective of him."

Speaking of true identity, I think we all have an idea of who Carrie really is."

"We just don't know that yet, Chuck. Let's get back to what we do know. I don't think the steps John took to help Nell and Paul were illegal. If something illegal was done, it would have been the steps taken by the mysterious computer person. Also, what John did was condoned by a member of the police department, Paul, and a member of child services, Nell. He will have acted with impunity."

"The business with the Prudhomme estate is quite another matter. It certainly appears that John stole money from the estate, although I can't picture him doing such a thing. He is a good person."

"What do we do about this?"

"We need to share what we know with Paul Tennyson. Of course, he knows about hiding the identity of the woman and child. He was a part of that. However, I don't believe he knows about the Prudhomme estate."

Paul was not happy that the Warners knew about his and Nell's part in the decisions made regarding Jackie Patnode and the child years ago. They had hoped that John would never divulge the truth. They both realized that their acts could, one day, come back to haunt them.

"What are you planning to do with this information?"

"Our only plan was to share this information with you and Nell in hopes that it would help us find Jackie and Carrie safe and sound. We are not interested in this information for any other reason."

"Since you know this much, I guess I should share something with you that I just learned a couple of hours ago. You would find out soon enough anyway because I will have to act on the information. The threatening letters sent to Carrie were written on the rectory computer." Both Chuck and Charles gasped in disbelief. "Similar threatening letters were sent to Jackie and to Maggie Scranton. They were also written on that computer. All the letters were sent to the state lab to be analyzed. There is no mistake where they came from."

"Why Maggie Scranton?" Charles questioned.

"Because she rents her garage apartment to Carrie. Now if you will excuse me, I have to visit the rectory."

Charles and Chuck headed to Carrie's apartment to share what they had just learned with Doug and Jane.

CHAPTER 91

JACKIE AND CARRIE WERE SURPRISED when they saw him enter the room again. He had already been there to bring food and water.

"Time to change your accommodations, ladies," he said. "People are getting too close to the truth. You will still be safe, but not as comfortable." He moved them to a subbasement of the house. It was the area where coal was stored in the days when coal was used as the primary heating fuel.

"Sorry there is no bathroom," he said. "You will have to solve the problem of taking care of that little issue. I am sure you will be creative. I will leave more food and water. Here are a couple of blankets. Don't want you to be cold." He did not tell them that the bathroom issue would not be important. That there would be no more food and water after this.

"Why are you doing this to us?" Carrie asked. "What do you want? Let us go, and we will say nothing."

He just stared at her. "You will never know," he said finally. He injected Jackie with the needle then headed for Carrie. She kicked him in the shin, but he was able to overpower her and administered the shot.

He left the house for the last time. *They will never be found*, he told himself. *The subbasement does not show up on the specs. I will let it be known around town that I have accepted a new position and will quietly leave town. John and Maude will be relieved.*

CHAPTER 92

John had no idea why Sgt. Tennyson was at the rectory to see him again. He was sure they had nothing more to discuss regarding church members. However, he asked Maude to leave the room after she ushered Paul into his office.

"John," Paul said, "some things have come to light since the disappearance of Jackie Patnode, and now Carrie Franklin, that we need to discuss. I am here to discuss what happened with the Prudhomme estate and the letters you wrote to Carrie Franklin, Jackie Patnode, and Maggie Scranton."

"I know nothing about any estate, or any letters."

"John, things will go easier for you if you don't deny these allegations. The Warner firm has investigated your involvement with the Prudhomme estate. There is no question that you took the money. Quite frankly, John, I am shocked and saddened by this. I would never have suspected this of you. There is no question that you wrote the letters to Jackie, Carrie, and Maggie. The state lab has proven that they came from your computer. John, I am not going to arrest you at this time, but you need to come down to headquarters to answer some questions."

John was visibly shaken. "Let me call Maude in. I need to explain to her what is happening."

"Go ahead, call her in, but let me explain everything to her," Paul said gently. "It might make things easier."

Maude listened quietly to Paul with her body shaking and her lips quivering.

"John did not write those letters, I did. I had to protect my husband."

"Maude, do not lie to protect me. I know all this can be straightened out soon."

"I am not lying, John. I did write the letters. Worse than that, I have found ways to listen in to your meetings with Paul, Nell, the Warners, and others you met with in your office, and have reported that information to your brother."

"Why, Maude?"

"Michael told me how you took money from the Prudhomme estate that was left for relatives to care for her cat and put it in a dummy corporation for your own financial benefit.

"Maude, how you believe that of me after thirty-five years of marriage?"

"I didn't at first, not until Michael showed me the financial statements and proof of the dummy corporation you set up in a false name." Maude started to cry hysterically.

"Maude, calm down. Michael was lying, probably to cover for something he has done himself."

"Michael and I have been working together to protect you."

"How?"

"By keeping in communication with each other. I have reported anything I heard in the rectory to him, so he can keep you from getting into trouble. He says he knows of other things you have done that was illegal. He said if I did not do this, he would expose something you did years ago that would cause you to lose your job and your good name."

"Paul, I need to explain something to you and Maude. Many years ago, I, with others from this community, took some steps to hide the identity of a young woman found in the old house on Brook Street. We took similar steps to hide a young child. We felt it was the right thing to do at the time. This probably was not a good thing to do. I have dreaded having this found out for years. Michael found out about this and has held it over my head for years."

"John, I need time to think about this new information. Settle the question of the letters right now," Paul interrupted. "John, write a sample of one of the letters you wrote. Maude, you do the same." They both got paper and pen and began to write.

John wrote a short note in cursive; Maude wrote a letter in block print. The letter was a carbon copy of the first letter Jackie had received. Paul took a copy of the letter Jackie had received and placed it beside what Maud had just written for John to compare.

"John," Paul said, "I now know you did not write the letters. I believe Maude when she said she was coerced into writing those letters. That makes other accusations against you suspect. I am not going to question you any further right now. I want to look further into other allegations against you.

"Maude, I am not sure right now how to handle the letter-writing situation. I know you did not do it under your own free will. I need to think about things."

Paul left the office, and John and Maude held each other tightly.

CHAPTER 93

PAUL SAT DOWN WITH CHIEF Jacob to tell him about his interview with the Abbotts. "I know John did not write the letters," he explained to the chief. "Now I wonder about the other allegations."

"Why don't you see if you can get access to the house? I doubt if there is anything in there to help you, but it is worth a try."

Paul went to the Barker real estate office to get a key for the house on Brook Street. "I do have a key to the house," he said, "but it is now owned by Michael Abbott. You should probably get his permission before going inside."

"Sure, go ahead in," Michael said. He was confident he had removed all traces of the women being in the basement. They did not know about the subbasement. "You won't find much. The house needs so much repair that I have decided to have a demolition crew come in in a few days and take it down. When I return from my new job orientation, I will talk to contractors about constructing a new building on the site then submit the plans to the town for approval."

He sure is a smooth talker, Paul thought. *I wonder if he means anything he is saying.*

Paul and his men went through the house with a fine-tooth comb. They investigated every room. They looked into closets, went through cupboards and drawers, and looked through the attic, basement, and garage. They found nothing of interest. "This is a dead end," he told his men. "I can't imagine where those two women are."

Carrie thought she heard sounds in the house, but she could do nothing in her drug-induced state.

That evening, Paul met with Jane, Doug, Maggie, and the Warners.

"I had a handwriting expert compare a sample of John Abbott's handwriting with the writing on the papers John supposedly signed on the Prudhomme estate. The writing did not match. The expert is convinced that John was not the person who completed that paperwork."

"I am so relieved to hear that," Maggie stated. "Maude and John are very nice people. I have a hard time believing either of them would be involved in anything nefarious."

"I believe," Paul told the group, "that Michael, John's brother, set John up for a fall. I just can't understand why. He received no benefit, no financial gain from the ploy, especially after purchasing the property himself. Now he wants to demolish the house."

"He can't!" Chuck shouted. "I know Carrie is in that building somewhere."

"Chuck," Paul said, "if Carrie had been in there, my men and I would have found her. We did a very thorough search."

"There is something we are missing," Chuck said. "I will check the plans of similar houses in the area that were built about the same time that house was. There has got to be something we are missing."

Joan's heart broke for her son. She knew his search would be fruitless.

CHAPTER 94

Nora Ryan was worried about Chuck Warner. He usually presented himself as a handsome, self-confident, but unpretentious young man. This morning, he looked haggard and worried. She watched as he looked through plans and records of houses built in Bellfield many decades ago. When he didn't find what he wanted, he would throw the papers down on the table in a harried manner and grab another one. He was obviously worried about something.

Nora went to the table where Chuck was working and said, "Can I help you find what you are looking for?"

"Probably not. I am looking at plans of old houses that might have an undetected space or room where something"—he did not want to say someone—"could be hidden. I can't tell you why right now, but it is very necessary that I find this information. I just can't find what I am looking for."

"Have you considered the subbasements of these old houses?"

"Subbasements?"

"Yes, most old houses had a small room or space under the basement to store coal for their coal furnaces."

Chuck jumped up from the table and hugged Nora. "Nora, that's it! That is what I have been looking for." He ran out of the building forgetting to return the plans he had been looking at to the shelves where the belonged. Nora gladly returned them for him.

Chuck called Paul from his cell phone. "I think I have the answer I have been searching for." He told Paul about the coal bins. "They are not shown on any building plans, but according to Nora Ryan most old houses have them. We need to get to Brook Street right now before demolition starts."

"Chuck," Paul said solemnly, "demolition started about an hour ago."

Carrie woke up to a very frightening noise. She was petrified. She could hear crews working on the house. She could hear parts of the roof and walls come crumbling down. She tried to wake Jackie. "Jackie! Wake up!" she shouted. "We have to find a way out of here. I think they are beginning to tear the house down." Jackie did not stir.

Carrie was sobbing. She did not want to die here. She knew now that she was in love with Chuck Warner. She thought that with Scott's help she could begin to develop a close relationship with him. She believed Chuck loved her too. She saw a small hole in the wall, but it was too small to crawl through. Besides, she would not leave Jackie. *Why do I feel such a close bond with this woman?* she asked herself. *It is not just because of our containment here,* she thought. *I have felt something special for her ever since we met and started working together.* In desperation, she threw her shoe through the hole in the wall.

Chuck was desperately running around, trying to get the attention of the driver of the bulldozer. He was not having any success. As he ran toward the house, he saw the shoe.

"Paul!" he screamed. "They are in here. This is Carrie's shoe. If we don't stop this demolition, both of them will be killed."

Paul had also been trying to get the attention of the driver of the bulldozer. He was not having any more success than Chuck. The driver was wearing headphones to lessen the noise of the demolition, and he was focused on what he was doing. He did not hear the two men, who were trying desperately to get him to stop his work.

When Paul heard Chuck scream and saw the shoe, he ran to his car and turned on the blue lights and the siren. The startled crane driver stopped what he was doing to see what the commotion was all about.

CHAPTER 95

Carrie and Jackie were pulled from the basement and rushed to the hospital. They had to be treated for dehydration and mild starvation. Carrie also had some minor injuries she had sustained trying to find a way out of the basement.

Paul had immediately made arrangements for Jackie to be returned to the rehab center to begin treatment for withdrawal for the drugs that had been administered to her for nearly two weeks.

Carrie had never used alcohol, never smoked, and never used drugs. For that reason, the doctors believed they could successfully treat her at the hospital for the drugs that she had been given the last few days. They did warn her that the treatment could cause her some significant pain during the withdrawal process.

Doug, Jane, and Chuck stayed by Carrie's side as she was being treated by the doctors. She slept most of the time, but became alert when emergency personnel came into the room to get Jackie ready to be taken to the ambulance and moved to the rehab center. She looked toward the other bed in the room.

"Is that Jackie?" she asked Jane.

"It is."

"Where are they taking her? Why can't she stay here?"

"She is being taken to the ambulance," Jane explained, "to the rehab center where she was treated a few years ago."

Carrie started to tear up. "She doesn't want to go back there, she told me that—"

"Carrie," Doug said, "Jackie's current addiction is not her fault. She was given the drugs by force. The rehab center that knows her best is the place where she can recover the fastest."

Carrie started to sit up. "I want to say goodbye to her."

"Whoa," said the EMT, "lie back down. We will wheel the bed over to you, so the two of you can say your goodbyes."

The EMT wheeled Jackie's bed close to Carrie's. One of them, who could read the raw emotion in both women's eyes, took a hand of each and clasped them together.

"Goodbye, Jackie," Carrie said, "get better soon and come back to Bellfield. I love you."

"I will," Jackie replied, "you take care of yourself. I love you too." Jackie's voice was so weak, that everyone in the room could barely make out what she was saying, But her meaning was palpable.

There were tears in both Jackie's and Carrie's eyes when the EMT said it was time to take Jackie down to the ambulance.

There were tears in Jane's eyes too.

Doug, Jane, and Chuck had decided not to tell Carrie what they had learned until she got stronger.

CHAPTER 96

MICHAEL DROVE TO THE BROOK Street property to see how the demolition of the house was progressing. He did not want it to appear that he was rushing out of town, but he needed to be gone before the cleanup began. He knew the cleanup crew would find the bodies. He planned to drive to the train station in Brattleboro, Vermont, take the train down to Hartford, Connecticut, then on to New York City where he could easily get lost in the crowd.

As he approached the house, he was shocked to find that the demolition work had stopped. He was even more shocked to see ambulances and a heavy police presence at the site. How could they have gotten out?

He quickly drove back to the motel room. He wanted it to appear that everything was normal, so when the maid came in to complete room service, he greeted her pleasantly, closed down his computer, and went out for coffee. This was their daily routine. When he believed it was time for room service, he would get out his computer and place it on his desk, giving the impression that he was working, then leave the room so she could complete her chores. If asked, the maid would report that Mr. Abbott followed his normal routine this morning, and appeared to be his usual self.

When Michael left the room, he did not check out. He wanted it to appear that he would be returning to the motel.

Paul waited at the hospital, hoping that either Carrie or Jackie would be able to say something that would give him an idea as to what had happened to them.

Jane was sitting by Carrie's bed, holding her hand. Doug and Chuck were standing nearby.

"Carrie," Jane said softly, "why were you in the basement of that house?"

Carrie opened her eyes. "Michael Abbott brought me there. He already had Jackie."

Upon hearing this, Chuck grabbed his cell phone and called Paul.

Michael slumped over the steering wheel of his car when he was pulled over by a state trooper, then saw Paul Tennyson pull up in back of the state trooper. Paul immediately put Michael under arrest for kidnapping and drugging Jackie and Carrie.

"I had a feeling my luck was running out," he told Paul.

The next morning, Michael agreed to plead guilty of kidnapping Carrie and Jackie. "First, I want to tell you why I did the things I did. Maybe then you will understand and not judge me too harshly. Also, I want my brother to be here. I want him to understand why Maude did the things she did. She really was not to blame. I frightened her into her actions. She needs to be exonerated in John's eyes." When the three men—Michael, John, and Paul—were seated comfortably in Paul's office, Michael began to speak.

"Twenty years ago, I was obsessed with Pat Lawrence. I think I was in love with her. That all changed when she became involved with Rick Reardon.

"Then I began to notice her sister, Donna. If I could not have one sister, I would take the other. When Donna's fiancé was killed, and her child was born, I saw a chance to get myself noticed by her. I tried to offer her fatherly advice and help. She always turned down my offers until she learned she would not receive financial assistance from the military for the upbringing of her daughter. She and her lover were never married, and she could not provide concrete proof that the child was his. I saw that as my chance to get into Donna's good graces. I provided financial assistance when she needed it, though I could tell that she was reluctant to accept my help.

"Donna continued to reject my romantic advances and finally told me that she could no longer accept financial assistance from me. I knew she was writing the amount of money I advanced to her in a ledger each time I gave her the money. She had every intention of paying me back in full as soon as she was able to do so. I also realized she wanted to end our relationship. I couldn't let that happen.

"That was when I started to put small amounts of drugs in her coffee, soda, or whatever she might have been drinking at the time. The drugs made her feel ill. It did not help with my romantic intentions, but it did allow me to continue visiting the household. She accepted my help when she felt too ill to care for the child properly.

"I am, of course, very ashamed to admit this, but as Donna became more and more ill from the drugs, my romantic interest in her waned. This interest turned to the child.

"I never intended to hurt her, just to show her my affection for her. Like her mother, the little child turned away from my efforts to love her."

"One day, Donna came into the room and saw me with the child. And ordered me out of the house forever. I could not let that happen. I snuck back into the house later that day. It was actually early evening and administered enough drugs to almost cause a fatal overdose. I then turned my attention to the child. Fortunately, I came to my senses and stopped my actions before I could cause too much damage to the child. I gave her some cereal and milk and left the house. The next morning, she was found on the steps by Maggie Scranton."

Michael put his head on the table and sobbed uncontrollably.

Ambulance sirens blared as it approached the rehab center with Jackie.

Carrie allowed Chuck to place his hand over hers.

CHAPTER 97

"MICHAEL," PAUL SAID, "I THINK it is best to end this interview for now."

Paul went to the hospital to relate Michael's story to Jane, Doug, and Chuck. "I need to get a DNA sample from Carrie in order to confirm Michael's story," he told them. "I am convinced that Carrie is Jackie's daughter, and she is the child Maggie Scranton found on the steps of the house on Brook Street all those years ago. However, we need to have proof of all of this before we talk to Carrie."

"I will be right back," Jane said. When she returned to the room, she brought the glass Carrie had been sipping water from.

"Will this help?" she asked Paul.

"It will." Paul put the glass in an evidence bag and headed for the state police lab in Montpelier.

The next morning, Michael returned to the police station to continue his interview with Paul. This time he asked to have both Maude and John present for the interview.

"The morning after the child was found," Michael continued, "I went to John's office and overheard the phone call he was making to make arrangements to hide the identities of Donna and Melanie Lawrence. Melanie was the child's first name. I threatened to expose this conspiracy if he did not provide me with financial security. He has struggled to do this ever since."

Maude gasped. She now understood why money was always so tight even though John made a decent salary.

Michael went on with his confession. "When Donna returned to Bellfield, I of course knew who she was right away. I suspected who Carrie was, but did not know for sure. Donna's amnesia was helpful, but I knew I needed to take some steps to protect myself just in case her identity was discovered. I wrangled my way into the good graces of the Prudhommes and convinced Emily to name me executor of her estate. I then set up dummy papers to indicate that John had stolen the money from the estate. I did such a good job that I even fooled Maude. At first, she did not believe it when I told her that John had taken the money. However, she could not argue with the paperwork I showed her. We planned to have Maude keep me informed of all pertinent events that occurred at the rectory. Maude believed that she was protecting John. You are very fortunate," he told his brother, "to have such a loving, faithful wife."

"We will talk about this later," John said to Maude in an angry voice.

"I even stole something," Maude admitted to Paul. "I took a pearl necklace from the Unique Boutique in hopes that Carrie would be accused of stealing and be fired. I wanted her to leave town. I didn't understand why she had come here to Bellfield. I was afraid her coming here was related to what John had done. She said she was looking for a cousin. I was afraid that she was a relative of the Prudhommes. Michael had told me that he believed she was a foster child. I just wasn't sure he was right, and could not take a chance that he was not right. I returned the pearls when I realized that Carrie was staying in town."

Paul said, "I may have to file charges against you for theft, Maude. I just don't know yet."

Maude nodded. She understood that that may happen.

CHAPTER 98

A WEEK AFTER MICHAEL'S ARREST, PAUL received the results of Carrie's DNA test. The results proved unequivocally that Carrie was Donna Lawrence's daughter, Melanie. Paul shared the information with Jane and Doug. They decided to discuss with Chuck and Scott Wynters the best way to inform Carrie of her heritage.

"Carrie's a very strong woman," Scott said. "It will, of course, take her some time to process this information. I will continue to see her through this processing period. Then I think she will be ready to be discharged from treatment. She has made excellent progress. She has come a long way. She has been able to alleviate many of her fears. Much of that is thanks to you, Doug and Jane, for your love and understanding. Your patience has allowed Carrie to develop the sense that touch is not evil, that being touched will not cause pain. I believe, in time, she will be able to develop normal, loving relationships."

Chuck sighed a sigh of relief.

"I want to be the one to tell Carrie about her life as a toddler," Jane said softly.

"I believe you are the best person to do this," Scott agreed.

Carrie was discharged from the hospital after spending just two days and one night there. The doctors told her not to return to work until she had at least two days' rest.

"Where is Dad?" Carrie asked Jane when she arrived at her apartment. Much to their delight, Carrie had started calling her foster parents Mom and Dad instead of Jane and Doug. Previously, she had vacillated between the two names. *I hope she is strong enough to digest all that I have to tell her*, Jane thought.

"Your dad decided to go to the range to hit golf balls. He is afraid his game will get rusty if he doesn't practice more. God forbid that happens." Jane laughed. "Let's make some coffee and sit down," Jane suggested. We need to talk."

Carrie listened intently, sometimes with tears in her eyes, as Jane told her about her past. She used the name of Donna Lawrence instead of Jackie Patnode when she told her about her biological mother. She began the story by telling her the history of the Lawrence family, including the relationship between Pat Lawrence and Rick Reardon.

Carrie interrupted, "Is the girl who came into the store to see Rick my cousin?"

Jane nodded.

Jane went on to tell Carrie about Michael Abbott's obsession with Pat, then Donna, then Carrie herself. She did not mention Carrie's given name.

"Michael's actions are the reason you have difficulty trusting people who have come into your life, especially people who love you."

A picture of Chuck came into Carrie's mind when Jane mentioned the word *love*.

"Scott will continue to work with you to help you build trust for the people around you. Michael will spend most of the rest of his life incarcerated. It is very important for you to understand that until Michael began drugging her, Donna Lawrence was a wonderful, loving mother. You must know that. You have happy memories of going to the playground and doing other things with her until Michael made her ill."

"Apparently, my biological father is buried somewhere here in the Bellfield cemetery," Carrie said. Jane nodded.

"Where is my biological mother?"

"She is currently recovering in a drug recovery center," Jane said softly.

"Oh god, are you telling me that Jackie Patnode, Donna Lawrence, is my real mother?"

Carrie sobbed uncontrollably as Jane held her in her arms.

EPILOGUE

Eighteen Months Later

Charles and Joan Warner would have liked to have had a large church wedding with many of their friends and clients invited, but understood why Carrie and Chuck preferred a small, quiet, and dignified ceremony at John's church with only their closest family and friends in attendance. John would, of course, officiate. The reception would take place in Friendship Hall where Carrie first attended church socials with Maggie. Joan, Jane, and Donna had made arrangements for the Star Restaurant to cater a simple luncheon after the ceremony.

As soon as other guests were seated, Charles and Joan Warner took their places on the right side of the church. Next, Paul Tennyson proudly ushered Jane and Donna down the aisle to their seats. They held hands tightly as a beautiful, glowing Carrie was walked down the aisle by a proud Doug. Scott Wynters was Chuck's best man, and Nan Wynters was Carrie's matron of honor. There were no other attendants.

Maggie and Nora had told the three mothers that they would check to see if everything for the luncheon was ready, so they would not have to worry about the details of the reception while pictures were being taken and while they received congratulations from their guests. They were excited about the story they would have to tell at their next ladies' luncheon. A tradition that would continue for many more years.

Maude was in attendance, but she stayed quietly in the background. She and John were still having difficulty resolving their differences. John could not reconcile the fact that Maude believed him capable of the things Michael had accused him of doing.

Rick and Nancy Reardon would be moving from Bellfield shortly after the wedding ceremony. They were working hard on strengthening their marriage. They realized they still loved each other despite their years of estrangement. They believed that living in a new environment, away from the constant reminder if Rick's indiscretion, would help them with this goal.

Donna Lawrence would manage the Unique Boutique in Bellfield. The Reardons planned to start a new store in Tempe, Arizona, where they would be living. Carrie would assist Donna in the running of the store.

"I hope this will be a temporary position," Chuck told his dad when he heard of this new arrangement. "I hope Carrie will soon be a full-time mom." The Waters and the Warners were excited about becoming grandparents. Donna was not sure she was ready to be a grandmother. *I hardly had time to be a mom,* she thought.

Pat and Jenny Lawrence were also at the wedding. Pat was escorted by David Donovan. She had finally told him about her past and who Jenny's father really was. He was aghast that Pat had not trusted him enough to tell him her story when they first met. He was hoping theirs would be the next wedding. Jenny was looking forward to going to college in the fall. She was happy her mom would not be alone. She was surprised to learn that Rick was paying part of her college expenses. She had made the decision not to pursue a relationship with him for the sake of both her mom and Rick and Nancy Reardon.

She was excited that Carrie was her cousin. They planned to spend some time together when Carrie and Chuck returned home from their honeymoon. Pat and Donna met for lunch, trying to get reacquainted. Right now, their relationship was tenuous at best.

Nell and her husband had moved to Florida, but they kept abreast of what was happening in Bellfield through contact with both Paul and Charles.

Michael was serving his time in the state prison

At the end of a moving ceremony, John said to Chuck, "You may kiss the bride."

There was not a dry eye in the church when John turned Carrie and Chuck toward the congregation and said, "Ladies and gentlemen, may I present Mr. and Mrs. Charles Warner Junior."

As she walked to the back of the church on Chuck's arm, Carrie thought, *I now know who I am.*

ABOUT THE AUTHOR

Norma A. Wyman has lived her entire life in small communities in southwestern New Hampshire. She married young and was a stay-at-home mom. When her two daughters entered elementary school, she enrolled in Keene State college. She was awarded a bachelor of science degree for education in 1967 and a master's degree for special education in 1977.

During her many years as an educator, she taught elementary school students, then later taught middle-grade students with behavioral and learning difficulties.

She also served as a Title One coordinator and a learning-disabilities specialist in a local school system.

After retiring from teaching in the public school system, she worked for ten years with incarcerated adults in a local corrections facility.

She later worked as a substitute teacher.

She has in the past, and continues to the present, to work with adults and children on a volunteer basis, helping them to develop reading and language arts skills.

Norma has always had an interest in writing (she won an award for an essay in high school). *Conspiracy* is her second novel. Her first, *Felony*, was published in June 2015.

Norma continues to live in a small community in southwestern Hew Hampshire.

CPSIA information can be obtained
at www.ICGtesting.com
Printed in the USA
BVHW070616060421
604308BV00002B/157